Blue Light

Gary Paulsen is the distinguished author of numerous books, ranging from Westerns to DIY. He has received great acclaim and many awards for his novels written for young people. *Hatchet* and its sequel, *Hatchet: The Return*, are among his best-known works. He has also written *Tasting the Thunder*, *The Fourteenth Summer*, *Ice Race* and *Nightjohn*, all available from Macmillan Children's Books.

He lives with his family in New Mexico, USA. He has sailed the Pacific and competed in the gruelling 1,049 mile Iditarod dog-sled race across Alaska.

BLUE LIGHT

Gary Paulsen

MACMILLAN
CHILDREN'S BOOKS

First published 1998 as The Transall Saga by Bantam Doubleday Dell, USA

First published in the UK 1999 by Macmillan Children's Books

This edition published 1999 by Macmillan Children's Books
a division of Macmillan Publishers Limited
25 Eccleston Place, London SW1W 9NF
Basingstoke and Oxford
www.macmillan.co.uk

Associated companies throughout the world

ISBN 0 330 37260 2

1 3 5 7 9 8 6 4 2

A CIP catalogue record for this book is available from
the British Library.

Typeset by SX Composing DTP, Rayleigh, Essex
Printed and bound in Great Britain by Mackays of Chatham plc, Kent

Blue Light

part

1

chapter 1

The desert was unusually quiet. A gentle breeze tumbled over the sparse vegetation along the wide canyon floor and then continued on its way to the north.

Thirteen-year-old Mark Harrison sat on a white slab of shale studying a small army of ants that was carrying off the crumbs that had dropped from a granola bar he'd just eaten.

A roadrunner, unaware of his presence, trotted to the base of the rock and stopped near a crimson cactus flower. Mark shifted position and it scurried away in the opposite direction.

He yawned even though it wasn't late. The sun hadn't completely faded behind the blue-gray mountains to the west. Still, he had put in a long day. He'd walked farther that day than on any of the previous three days and he was ready to turn in.

His parents had given him just one short week to backpack across the old Magruder Missile Range. And if he didn't meet them at the appointed spot on the other side by

Saturday afternoon his mom had threatened to call out the National Guard.

Hiking and backpacking were Mark's one obsession. He saved every dime of his paper-route money to buy equipment and now he had some of the best. In his spare time he studied survival books and magazines to stay up on the latest techniques. But so far he had been allowed to hike only short, easy trails and had actually camped out only twice in his life. This time he'd hit the jackpot, though.

Mark stretched, ran his hand through his short brown hair and grabbed his bedroll and pack. He'd decided to make camp in the canyon. The quiet here was a little unnerving for a city boy, but there was a trickle of water, and a dead tree that protruded from the south wall would provide plenty of firewood.

When the small blaze was crackling and his bed was made, Mark stretched out on the soft down sleeping bag and stared up at the stars. This was the life he wanted for himself. Someday he'd fix it so that he was always camping under the wide-open skies.

He yawned again and was just about to settle in for the night when a flaming ball of fire shot over the edge of the canyon wall.

The fiery thing was the size of a grapefruit and glowed bright orange around its blue edges. It danced and sputtered when it touched the ground. Then it fizzled away to nothing.

Mark snapped on his flashlight and found his camera. He scrambled to the top of the dirt wall and peeked over. To his right, behind a huge rectangular boulder, was a bright, iridescent beam of bluish white light that seemed to be projected at the ground from somewhere in the sky.

For a full minute he stood transfixed, watching the strange tube of light. It had two sections, each supercharged with electricity. The sides pushed mightily against each other, but both were equal in power, so nothing moved except for an occasional shooting spark caused by the tremendous friction.

He shook his head. This was worth looking into. Maybe it was some sort of experiment the air force had once conducted out here and then forgotten about, or maybe . . . He swallowed. Maybe it was something not from this planet at all.

Mark inched closer, snapping pictures as he went. When he reached the boulder he used his flashlight to search for a way up and began climbing.

The top of the big rock was flat. He pulled himself up and sat, staring again. The inside of the tube contained myriad surging colors: reds, blues and yellows. It was like watching a spectacular laser light show being performed just for him.

Slowly he put out his hand to see if the light generated heat. Too late, he heard the rattle—and felt the snake strike.

He jerked his hand back and leaped to his feet. The sudden movement threw him off balance and he fell, off the boulder and into the light.

chapter 2

The air was thick and humid and smelled of a coming rain. Mark opened his eyes. It was daytime but the sun seemed to be hidden by clouds, and everything was in shadow. His head was pounding and felt as if it weighed a ton.

He tried to remember. The light. There was the tube of blue light and then . . . the snake. He glanced at his hand, which was resting comfortably on his chest. It wasn't swollen at all. Even more curious, it didn't hurt.

Mark brought it closer. There were no marks anywhere from the rattler's bite. He flexed his fingers. They worked fine. It was as if nothing had happened. He dropped his arm and let it rest in the tall red grass beside him.

Grass? Red? Mark rubbed his temples. *I must be delirious,* he thought. He turned his head. Trees. There were trees here. So many that they blocked his view of the sky. Their leaves were a dull burnt red like the tall grass and the tangled brush that surrounded them.

Something's wrong. Mark pulled himself to a sitting position. He'd read about this, about snakebite and what happened. *It must be the snake venom. It's gone to my head and now I'm having hallucinations.*

He took a deep breath and stood up. The sandy desert landscape was gone. It had changed to dense jungle. The canyon he had camped in the night before was nowhere in sight. The boulder and the blue light were gone too. Nothing looked the same.

A snorting sound came from beyond the trees. A large hairy animal resembling a buffalo charged into the small opening. It had long tusks, beady eyes and a piglike snout. The thing waved its shaggy head back and forth, sniffed the air and bellowed.

This can't be happening. Mark edged toward the nearest tree. The instant he moved, the beast spotted him. It pawed the ground with its large hooves and lowered its massive head to attack.

There was no time to think. Mark jumped for the closest branch and swung up into the tree just as the sharp tusks rushed underneath him. The animal stopped and sniffed the air again. Unable to locate its victim, the creature snorted and ambled off into the red forest.

Mark stayed on the branch. He was shaking and his mind was in a whirl. "All right. Would a hallucination attack me? This must be a real place," he whispered. "But where is it? And how did I get here?"

He thought back to the night before and the energy-charged light. *It has to be. Whatever that blue light was, it's the key. When I fell into the tube it transported me to . . . to where? I don't even know if I'm on Earth anymore.*

An empty feeling in his stomach let him know that it was

past breakfast. He shrugged it off and continued to reason with himself. *Okay, I'm in another world, possibly on another planet. One with red rubbery leaves and weird-looking animals. But I'm still me. My clothes are the same. I still get hungry. So what do I do now?*

He glanced around to make sure the buffalo creature was gone, and slid down from the tree. *The thing to do . . .* For a full half minute nothing came. No idea. Then he shrugged. *The thing to do . . . is look around. Let's see what we're dealing with here.*

Walking was difficult. The brush was thick and snarled in knots and tore at his jeans legs. Seeing more than a few feet ahead was impossible except in an occasional clearing.

It was raining now. It sounded like a heavy rain but the drops were barely able to penetrate the canopy. Only a few landed on the ground around him.

He stuck out his tongue and caught a drop on the tip. It didn't taste like the rain back home. This stuff was bitter. It also smelled like the medicine his mother made him take when he had the flu.

Shaking his head, he pulled his compass from his jeans pocket. The needle spun wildly, then settled on a direction to his right. He shoved the compass back into his pocket.

"For the sake of argument"—it made him feel better to talk aloud—"let's say there is a north here. Then if I keep going this way . . ." He took two steps and found himself in gooey red mud up to his knees. He tried to climb out but every time he moved, it sucked him down.

Quicksand.

No . . . Don't panic. You know about this. Remember, you read about it in Hiker *magazine.*

8

The red ooze quickly reached his thighs and continued to pull him down.

Okay . . . flat. That's it. Don't fight, remember. Get flat and swim your way out, pushing the muck away from your face. He took a breath and fell over on his stomach. The mud instantly grabbed at his clothing, glued itself to his face and dragged him under. His whole body was now covered with the slime.

Using every ounce of strength, Mark struggled against the mud but the precious few inches he managed to gain were quickly lost as he was sucked down again.

He couldn't breathe. Wildly he threw out his arms, trying to reach above him with his fingers.

His left hand caught something solid near the edge of the pit. A root. He pulled and when his head cleared the top he gulped in air. Using his other hand, he grabbed some underbrush and kept tugging until finally his upper body was resting on solid ground.

He wiped at the slime blocking his nostrils, took a deep, raspy breath and dragged his legs out. He was too tired to get up. Rolling onto his side, he curled up in the thicket and closed his eyes.

Above him the red leaves in the trees rustled. Something soft and warm plopped on his forehead. He opened his eyes. There were birds up there. Reaching for a fistful of grass, he wiped the bird poop off his muddy face without taking his eyes off the trees. It was hard to spot the birds because they were the same color as the leaves, but the longer he stared, the clearer they became. They had wide feathers the same shape as the leaves and long brownish beaks that blended with the branches.

At least something lives in this stupid place besides that buffalo thing. Mark inched to his feet. The slimy red mud dropped off him in clods, leaving a thick drippy goo clinging to his skin and clothes.

He was exhausted and his mouth was dry from sucking air. *Water. If I'm going to survive this . . . dream . . . or whatever it is, I need to find water.*

Careful to skirt the quicksand, Mark made his way through a wall of brush to a large red meadow of tall wavy grass where he could actually see patches of sky. But instead of the bright blue color that had been there yesterday the sky was a hazy yellow.

A rabbitlike creature with long, curly hair hopped across the clearing on its hind legs like a kangaroo. When it saw him the fuzzy thing bounced away.

Mark watched the animal disappear. *I feel like Alice in Wonderland. All I need now is to find the Mad Hatter.*

The sudden rain had left shallow puddles in a few places across the meadow. Mark dropped to his knees and scooped the bitter liquid into his mouth. It was the only water available so it would have to do. *Maybe,* he thought, not at all sure of the answer, *maybe it won't kill me.*

He drank until his sides hurt and his stomach threatened to send it all rushing back up. Then he fell into the tall grass to rest. Maybe he'd just stay here a while . . . take a nap . . . or—

His back was on fire. He leaped to his feet and began swatting wildly at his skin. Now his arms and legs were burning too. Tubular, scorpionlike insects with antennas and long pincers swarmed over him, biting small chunks out of his skin. It felt as if they were eating him alive.

Mark ripped off his shirt, shook it and used it to try to scrape them off. The bugs didn't want to let go. They hung on to his flesh with both pincers. He smashed those he could reach with his hand. Some had to be pulled off, along with tiny pieces of his flesh.

Between the cracks in the red mud on his skin, huge pink welts grew, covering his back, neck, chest and arms.

To make doubly sure he had all the bugs off, Mark ran to a tree and scraped his back against it. Then he removed his boots, jeans and shirt and the rest of his clothes.

Laying his pocketknife, matches and compass aside, he picked up his jeans and shook them vigorously. When he was positive his pants were bug free, he gingerly put his foot into one leg.

Behind him he heard a familiar deep roar. He stiffened. Without looking, he dropped the jeans and raced behind the tree.

The buffalo creature rammed the trunk in front of Mark. Birds spewed out from the branches, making loud screaming noises. The commotion didn't stop the creature. It backed up a few steps, then charged again, continuing to ram the tree until one of its long tusks became lodged in a crack.

Mark used the opportunity to escape into the dense brush at the other side of the clearing. By the time the beast had dislodged itself, Mark was sitting safely in the lower branches of another tree.

The creature sniffed the air. It had lost its prey again. The thing angrily stomped around the tree until it discovered Mark's shirt and ripped it to shreds. Then it started on one of his hiking boots.

"No!" Mark yelled. "I need those."

The beast stopped. It blew out snot and trotted to the center of the meadow with the boot still in its teeth.

The stupid thing can't see more than about ten feet, Mark thought. He carefully climbed down the tree and slowly moved behind another one. Keeping trees between himself and the beast, he managed to circle the meadow.

Finally the animal gave up hunting for him and crashed back into the forest.

Mark ran to his clothes. His shirt was a rag. One boot was missing and his jeans had been ground two inches into the wet soil.

chapter 3

Mark slumped against the tree. He was still in his underwear and socks, clutching his meager possessions. They included a pair of torn, filthy jeans, a belt, one boot, a broken compass, a watch, a smashed box of splintered matches, a knife and the tattered cloth that had been his shirt.

The bug bites were beginning to itch. He was hungry and miserable. Closing his eyes as tight as he could, he willed this awful place and all the strange things in it to go away.

He opened his eyes. Nothing had changed. Wherever he was, this was reality. He was alone in this bizarre land and if he wanted to stay alive he would have to find ways to feed and take care of himself.

Snatching some of the red grass, he held it up to his nose. It smelled like grass even though it was the wrong color. Hesitantly, he put a little in his mouth. It tasted like grass too. He spat it out.

Mark scraped the mud off his watch. It had stopped working. His stomach told him that if time in this place was anywhere near the same as on Earth, it was just after noon and he'd already missed two meals.

At home his parents were probably eating lunch about now. Thinking about his parents made him feel more alone. They wouldn't know he was missing for another two and a half days. And then what? Even if his mom called out half the army reserves, they'd never find him. Not here. Not in this primitive world that was accessible only through the strange energy tube.

"Well, hotshot," Mark said, sighing. "You wanted to live by yourself . . ."

Resting his chin on his knees, he listened to the jungle noises around him. The trees creaked and the large flat leaves swayed in the breeze. There was an occasional shrieking sound he recognized as birdcalls.

He sighed again, then stood up and warily pulled on his filthy, damp jeans. Not wanting to ruin his socks, he took them off and stuffed them in his remaining boot, along with what was left of his shirt. Then he put his knife, matches and compass in his pocket and started walking.

His plan was to keep going until something better than what he'd already seen presented itself.

It didn't.

The jungle grew darker, more tangled and more overgrown. Vines hung snakelike from the trees all around him. Grotesque lizards with abnormally large heads darted in and out of the foliage. And there was a new sound. In the tops of the now almost black trees, he could hear animals chattering. They made a clicking noise like stone hitting stone.

Squinting, he scanned the branches overhead. Twice he

thought he saw something move but couldn't quite make out what it was.

Mark wondered if he should go back to the meadow. He considered his position. At least there was water there. Here there was nothing.

A piercing howl cut through the darkness. The clicking stopped.

A shiver ran up Mark's back. He swallowed and waited. What now? Finally the chattering started again and he moved on.

Normally he was good at walking. It was something he prided himself on. He could walk for hours without resting. But this was different. His bare feet were being cut to ribbons by the coarse underbrush, and more important, he was hungry.

He decided to turn back. The meadow area was safer because he could see what was around him. Maybe he'd missed something there that he could eat. It was worth a try.

Just as he turned, the chattering sound came closer and grew to a deafening roar. Something hit the ground behind him. He spun around and received a crashing blow to the side of the head. A rock the size of his fist knocked him to his knees. Then came more rocks, pelting his body from every direction.

He covered his head and rolled into a ball.

Then, as suddenly as it had begun, the chattering stopped. So did the rocks.

Mark dropped one of his aching arms. He was bruised and sore but nothing felt broken. Above him he saw a flurry of motion. Swinging effortlessly from the branches were small, white, furry animals. He would have called them monkeys but they looked more like miniature teddy bears with long arms and tails.

One of them had stayed behind. With its sharp claws, it was clinging to a tree about halfway down the trunk, watching him.

"Get out of here," Mark yelled, reaching for one of the rocks.

The monkey creature clicked its tongue loudly, rebuking him. It moved up the tree, but only a few feet.

Mark drew his arm back to throw. He stopped. The object in his hand was heavy like a rock and it felt smooth and round. But it had some sort of outer layer. He shook it. The insides sloshed around. He tried to peel it but the skin was too tough.

There's got to be a way. Mark gathered an armful of the tree rocks and headed out of the darkness. When he reached the edge of the meadow he dropped his find in a pile and examined one of them. They were the color of the bark of the trees and resembled small coconuts.

Mark shook one again. *There's something in there.* He reached for his pocketknife. "Oh, please let it be good for food . . . ," he whispered.

There was a soft clicking a few feet behind him. Mark looked over his shoulder. The monkey-bear had followed him.

"Shoo. Go away." Mark tossed one of the tree rocks at it. Like lightning, the little creature's long arm shot up and caught it.

"Hey, that's pretty good." Mark turned back to what he'd been doing. He tried peeling the rock but only bits of the heavy skin would come off.

Something hit him in the shoulder. It was the tree rock. The monkey-bear had tossed it back.

"Cut that out. Can't you see I'm starving here?" He jabbed the knife into the top of the rock. Only the tip went in and he was afraid to push harder because he might damage the knife.

"I know there's got to be a way," he muttered. He took the rock to a nearby tree and pounded it against the trunk. Nothing. Disgusted, he threw it on the ground.

The monkey-bear waddled over, picked up the rock, inserted one of its razor-sharp claws in the middle and easily broke it open. A thick brown liquid spilled out. The little animal greedily slurped it up from both halves and then scooped out the dark meaty parts with its claws and shoved them in its mouth.

Mark raced to his pile of rocks. He felt for a soft spot in the center of one and jabbed his knife in. Gradually he worked the two sides apart. He lifted one of the halves to his lips and guzzled down the brown juice.

It had a pleasant taste—like milk, only sweeter. He drank the other half and then used his knife to dig out the meat. This part wasn't so great. It reminded him of bean sprouts and he thought about spitting it out. Instead he forced himself to swallow. It might be his only food source for a while.

He went through eleven of the rocks before he was satisfied. The meal made him feel better. Now maybe he could concentrate on something besides his stomach.

The light in the meadow was growing dim. Apparently this place had a night. He would have to choose a place to camp for the dark period. The thought of waking up to a buffalo creature—or whatever that howling thing was—

worried him. He definitely didn't want to sleep here in the open.

The dark part of the jungle didn't appeal to him much, either. In the end he compromised and decided to look for a spot just beyond the edge of the meadow.

He found a nice grassy place just inside the shadows and well hidden by the brush. He watched the monkey-bear waddle to a tree and shimmy up to a wide, flat branch the size of a small table. The animal stopped and looked at him expectantly.

Mark rubbed the back of his neck. "I don't know. I really hadn't thought about spending the night in a tree."

The monkey-bear clicked its tongue and jumped up and down.

"Oh, all right. I'll give it a try. I guess it would be a little harder for the bad ones to get to me up there—that is if I don't fall out and break my neck."

Getting to the lower branches was easy. He'd done that when the buffalo creature was after him. The middle part was a lot harder because the branches were farther apart. Mark tried a couple of times and gave up. The monkey-bear scurried up to the top limbs and waited.

Mark shook his head. "No thanks. This is high enough for me. You go on ahead." He wedged his boot, which still held his few possessions, in between the trunk and the branch and then stretched out on his stomach on the wide limb.

If I'm lucky, I'll wake up in the morning and this whole thing will all have been a dream. A bad dream, he thought as he dozed off.

chapter 4

The warm night was long. Mark dozed fit-
fully and woke every few hours to the strange noises of the
jungle. Twice he fell off his perch. Finally he discovered that
if he locked his legs around the limb he was less likely to
take a spill.

The blue light haunted his dreams. Half awake, he re-
called a similar energy force he'd read about once in science
class. It was a theory some scientist had about what would
happen if matter and antimatter ever actually met. Bits of
information came back to him, something about the massive
amount of power that would be produced and the way it
could affect life.

He didn't care about any of that, only that it had affected
his life and he wanted out of this place. Then, just as the
meadow began to fill with the hazy yellow light of a new
day, he jerked awake.

The tube of light. Of course—he had to find it again. It
was his way back to Earth and home. He grabbed his boot
and dropped to the ground.

Immediately fierce hunger pains shot through him. Eat. He had to eat, and the only place he knew where there was any food was in the dark jungle. The blue light would have to wait.

Mark tied his boot to his belt loop with the lace and started walking. The monkey-bear crawled down a vine and landed softly beside him.

"Where do you little guys keep your tree rocks, Willie?" The name just came. He seemed like a Willie. "You know what I'm talking about, like the ones your buddies tried to kill me with yesterday. There wouldn't happen to be a great big stash just lying around somewhere easy?"

Willie cocked his head and clicked his tongue.

Mark frowned. "I don't think we're doing too well in the communication department." He led the way into the shadowy jungle.

On this trip he paid more attention to the things he saw. The lizards were still there, and there were large flowering plants mixed in with the underbrush. He noticed that the trees in the dark jungle were different from the shorter ones closer to the meadow. Some were so tall he couldn't see the tops. This kind had smooth trunks with no low branches, and they usually had dozens of vines hanging from them.

A few yards inside the dark jungle he heard the clicking noise start. It didn't worry him this time. He was even prepared for the monkey-bears to bombard him with tree rocks. It would save him from going after them.

They didn't. Mark figured it had something to do with Willie, who clicked nonstop and stayed right with him.

It was getting almost too dark to see. Mark searched the tops of the trees above him.

They've got to be up there somewhere. I guess I'll have to climb. He yanked on one of the vines to see if it would hold his weight. It seemed sturdy enough. He jumped and tried to haul himself up but his arms were too weak and he slid back down.

I should have paid more attention to rope climbing in gym class. He moved to another vine. This one was hanging closer to the trunk. He braced his bare feet against the smooth bark, and using the vine for leverage, he slowly walked up the tree at an angle.

Halfway up he glanced down and nearly lost his balance. He guessed it was more than a thirty-foot drop to the ground. A dizzy feeling washed over him and his palms began to sweat. He closed his eyes until the feeling passed; then he climbed again.

At the first limb he came to, he stopped. He sat for a long time just clinging to the vine and trying not to look down.

Willie had climbed past him and was clicking at him from the top branches. Mark looked up and saw him swinging back and forth from one limb to another. Above Willie, Mark spotted a cluster of tree rocks dangling from the end of a long branch and half hidden under the wide leaves.

He tied the vine around his waist and worked his way up to the next limb. Once he made it to the end of the long narrow branch, the tree rocks were easy to pick. He pulled off every one he could reach and let them fall to the ground.

With no warning there was a crack and Mark felt himself

falling. He grabbed at air, swung backward and jolted to a stop midway to the ground.

The vine he'd tied around his waist held. He fastened his arms around the closest limb and clung to it.

Willie crawled down to see what was going on.

"I think," Mark said, taking a deep breath, "that's probably enough shopping for one morning."

chapter 5

"*It could be anywhere.*" *Mark threw up* his hands. He had managed to find the clearing where he'd first awakened in the tall red grass. But the blue light didn't show itself.

His stomach made a loud rumbling sound. He was hungry all the time now. The tree rocks were good but they were mostly liquid and only took the edge off his appetite. He wanted something solid. Pizza. Pizza would be good. Thick crust smothered in three different kinds of melted cheese. He would kill for a pizza.

"Stupid." Hearing the word aloud caught him off guard. He said it again, slower. "Stupid. Daydreaming isn't going to get you anywhere. Think. Think about all the tons of stuff you read in those how-to-stay-alive books. Use it."

Mark concentrated. The problem was all those books were for Earth. He was sure he had come to another planet—Earth-like, perhaps, but so strange. Still, some things would work. The handbooks all said to check out the surroundings. Food was usually not too far away. Bugs were always handy. He made a face. The fire bugs deserved to be food but how would you eat them without ripping your tongue out? Okay, what else? The screaming birds. No, too difficult. Maybe later, after he had more time to think and plan and get some kind of weapon. The fat-head lizards. They were slow and would be easy to catch. But then what? He'd have to figure out a way to cook them. And what if they were poisonous? What if *anything* was poisonous? No, he'd stick with convenience foods for now. Stuff he knew hadn't killed other animals. Life here seemed similar to Earth life. Food might work the same. Whatever other animals could eat, he could eat. Maybe.

What else had he read? There was the usual stuff on keeping warm. He rubbed his bare arms. Unless the weather changed he wouldn't have to worry about that. Shelter. He really didn't need a house but he didn't want to sleep on that stupid limb forever, either.

He opened a tree rock as he walked back toward the big meadow. His spirits were higher and the ideas kept coming. Until he located the light, he would live next to the dark jungle, because that was where the tree rocks were, and the buffalo creatures didn't seem to go there. And, of course, there was Willie. It was nice to have company.

In the meantime, he would make circles, wider and wider every day, hoping to find the mysterious blue light.

chapter **6**

The fire bugs had been easy to collect. The only trick was making sure none of them got on his skin while he was concentrating on catching the others.

Mark had eased up to the outer edge of a colony and picked off the stragglers. With his knife he sliced their pincered heads off, stabbed them through the middle and deposited them safely in a sock.

For lunch he had four tree rocks and more than a dozen of the long crunchy insects. The first one was the hardest to swallow. His mind and his stomach fought over the idea until the hunger pains won out. He closed his eyes and pretended he was munching on the trail mix he'd packed for his hike.

"Break's over." Mark tied a knot in the top of his bug sock and dropped it on his dwindling pile of tree rocks. "Back to work, Willie." The monkey-bear slapped the ground with his thick black palms and followed Mark to a tree just inside the dark part of the jungle.

Mark had chosen this particular tree because it had two

strong limbs that forked into a perfect **V**. For the better part of the morning he had been hauling dead branches to his tree and arranging them across the two limbs to form a floor.

When the branches were fitted together as closely as possible, he went to the edge of the meadow and broke off long sticks from the tangled underbrush. Using a pattern he'd seen in an army survival manual, he wove the supple twigs into a loose mat and placed it on the floor.

"Almost finished. All we need now are some of those big rubbery leaves and presto, the master bedroom is complete. No more hitting the ground in the middle of the night. Come on, Willie. We'll get the leaves and some extra tree rocks for tomorrow, and then we'll have just enough time to make a small circle around the outskirts of the meadow."

Mark discovered that his eyes adjusted more quickly to the shadowy jungle this time. He even spotted a group of monkey-bears before they saw him. They were startled, and scrambled to the tops of the trees.

"I wish I could get up there that fast," Mark muttered. He chose a sturdy vine and began the long process of walking up the side of the tree.

Willie climbed over him, grabbed another vine and swung up into the branches of a tall tree.

Mark studied his vine. "There's got to be an easier way." He dropped to the ground. "An extension ladder would be good." He shrugged. "So would a helicopter."

He tied a loop near the bottom of the vine and put all his weight on it. It held. He tied another loop a little higher in another vine next to his and stepped into it. Back and forth he went, tying loops to create a makeshift ladder, until he had climbed into the low branches.

"Okay. Now what? There won't always be rocks in this tree. And I can't take my ladder to the next one." Mark scratched his head. He watched Willie swinging back and forth on the vines. It looked so easy.

Mark yanked on one of the higher vines, testing it. Before he could talk himself out of it, he pushed off.

It wasn't as bad as he'd imagined. Twice more he swung out, swept back and landed lightly on the limb. The third time he pushed off, he swung out halfway to the next tree, reached for another vine—and missed.

chapter 7

Everything on him hurt. Mark rolled to his side and nearly screamed. Something inside him had ripped apart.

A large flowering plant had helped to break his fall but every time he moved, even a fraction of an inch, searing pains racked his body.

He tried not to breathe, not to blink.

It was raining again. He could hear the soft, comforting sound of the drops hitting the leaves.

A drink of water, even the bitter stuff in the puddles, would taste good right now, he thought. *Get up. Get to the water.*

He forced himself to stand and nearly passed out from the pain. Taking short, ragged breaths only when absolutely necessary, he moved toward the meadow a few halting steps at a time.

Near his tree he lowered his aching body to a large puddle and drank. He could feel himself starting to fade.

With effort he stood and turned to look at his tree. There

was no way. If he tried to pull himself up to his bed, he might make the damage inside him worse.

He stumbled to the tall grass in the shadows, sank into it and allowed the blackness to take over.

◆ ◆ ◆

The clicking. It was high pitched and loud and next to his ear. *Make it stop,* he thought.

He groggily opened his eyes and stared dully into Willie's furry, round face. The monkey-bear squealed and patted Mark's head.

"You haven't got any aspirin, have you?" Mark sat up, his breath hissing with pain. It was his ribs. Maybe he'd cracked one—or more. He'd heard somewhere that cracked ribs hurt like blazes when you took a breath. He had to tape them up in some way.

He felt inside his boot for his tattered shirt, tore it into strips and tied the pieces together. Then he wrapped the makeshift bandage tightly around his ribs. They still hurt, but the pain seemed more under control.

He was hungry. But then he was always hungry. Judging from the way his stomach was growling, he figured he had probably slept through a meal or two.

Next to his tree he could see his stack of tree rocks. Inching to his feet, he slowly made his way to the pile. His stash of fire bugs was still in the sock where he'd left it. He ate and lay back down.

Tomorrow he would have to find a new food source. The tree rocks were out of his reach for now. Scouting for the blue light was also out of the question for a while. He would

29

just have to take it easy and try to be patient until his ribs healed.

To take his mind off the pain, he forced himself to think about ways to make his existence here more bearable. When he was able, he would build a ladder for his tree house. And some kind of weapon would be nice, in case he ran into that howling thing on one of his trips into the dark jungle.

And food. It always came back to that. He had to eat.

He chewed on the end of a long piece of red grass. He wondered what his parents would do when they found out he was gone. He was their life. His mom was a member of the parents' club at school. She never missed a function and volunteered for everything. And his dad . . . his dad was so proud of his only son, he had established a college fund when Mark was a baby. He told all his friends that someday his son was going to be a doctor.

I could use a doctor right now, Mark thought. He closed his eyes and dreamed of going home.

chapter 8

Days turned into weeks. Mark didn't know how many. He did his best not to think so much about home, his parents and the way things had been, and tried instead to concentrate on the strange new world around him.

His ribs had been slow to heal. For weeks his diet had consisted mainly of a variety of insects. He'd managed to find a kind of bland-tasting grub worm that lived in the flowering plants and a jumping red bug that reminded him of the grasshoppers back home, only larger. Once in a while he was lucky enough to find a discarded tree rock that one of the monkey-bears had dropped in the dark jungle.

Now he was making circles again. He still was wearing his bandage and was careful not to push himself too hard, but scouting was important to him. If he wanted to go home, the blue light had to be found.

On one of his rounds he'd discovered a swamp of quicksand not too far into the dark jungle. If it hadn't been for a screaming bird that was stuck in it and fighting to get free, he might have stumbled into it himself.

Another time, on a round in the light jungle, he'd found a clear pool of water that came from an underground spring. Visiting the pool was a treat for him. It was his favorite part of every day. When he'd first seen his reflection in the pond it had startled him. The person looking up from the water was so skinny his bones stood out like a skeleton's—a dirty skeleton with shaggy, matted hair.

If he stood just right and looked through an open patch of jungle, beyond the pool he could see the peaks of distant mountains. He'd made up his mind to go there when he was completely well.

The tree house was much different now. In between hunting for food and scouting, Mark had fashioned a wooden ladder by securing rungs to two tall branches with vines. He had also added a second story, a small platform that held his food supplies.

He'd also put a lot of effort into weapons. The best one so far was a spear. It was a long straight pole with a finely carved point. Now he was working on a bow using a strong stick and the shoestring from his boot. He still hadn't made too much progress with it, and there didn't seem to be much straight wood for arrows.

He had to hunt for food, and he'd need skins for clothing when his jeans wore out, but he didn't seem to need weapons for defense. So far the animals in the area hadn't posed much of a threat. The buffalo creatures came around, but because of their poor eyesight Mark could easily hide from them. They represented a lot of meat, of course, but running up to one of them and sticking a spear in it bordered on suicide. Other animals didn't bother him, and except for occasional visits from Willie, the monkey-bears didn't want anything to do with him. To them he was just another animal in the jungle.

Twice, Mark had killed fat-head lizards. He had used some of his match tips to start a fire and had roasted his catch on the end of a green limb. The meat was a little grainy but they were the most filling meals he'd had since coming to the red forest.

Life was simple. Find food, scout the countryside, try to make new things and sleep.

Life was simple. Except that sometimes in the still of the night he could hear the faint call of the Howling Thing. And once at the pool he'd seen tracks that resembled dog prints—only bigger.

chapter 9

Whenever he went out now Mark took the spear. The sharpened point was four inches long, and it made him feel better to carry the weapon. His circles were getting larger and sometimes he was forced to spend the night away from his tree.

That day he had traveled quite a distance from home. Early that morning he had packed both socks and his boot with food, stopped by the pool for a long drink and then started out.

To anyone else the miles of red forest and never ending trees might have looked the same. But Mark was getting to be an expert at noticing differences. Earlier he had discovered a new meadow where the grass wasn't quite so red and was short and dry. The trees weren't as tall there either, and their leaves had an odd orange tint.

Mark continued on, listening for new sounds. His ears had become tuned to every noise in the jungle. He knew even small sounds like the breeze rippling through the grass.

Here, though, something was making him uncomfortable. It wasn't so much what he heard as the sounds he didn't hear. This part of the jungle was too still—not even the sound of birds.

Ahead of him a newly broken twig dangled from a larger branch. Mark stopped and searched the ground. There were no tracks but he could see where the grass had been pushed down by something that had recently passed through.

Raising his spear, Mark moved silently through the trees. Whatever was out there was close.

A horrible squeal broke the silence. Mark froze.

It was close. Somewhere in front of him.

He hustled up the nearest tree and waited.

Nothing came his way. Still, he waited. He'd learned not to take chances.

Finally the birds came back and the sounds in the forest returned to normal. Mark dropped to the ground and picked his way through the brush. Two hundred yards in front of him he saw another clearing with low grass. Staying in the cover of the trees, he listened. He couldn't shake the feeling that something was wrong.

The clearing was empty. It was dry, and light red like the last one except for one dark splotch of color on the other side.

Mark skirted the outside, staying well hidden in the brush. The dark color intrigued him. He reached down and touched it.

Blood.

Mark ducked back in the trees. Any animal that had lost that much blood had to be big. And what disturbed him even more was that whatever killed it had managed to carry the whole thing off without leaving even a tiny piece of the carcass.

Get away. He had to get away. There was no time to lose.

He turned and was about to rush back around the clearing when he spotted something in a tree.

Quietly, almost reverently, he walked to it and pulled it from the trunk.

It was an arrow.

chapter 10

Mark couldn't sleep. Before dawn, he was sitting on his mat in the tree house turning the arrow over and over in his hands. It had colorful black and red feathers from birds he'd never seen. The shaft was painted with a black zigzag design, and the point was made of a sharp, chiseled rock skillfully attached with a piece of water-shrunken leather.

Finding the arrow changed everything. It meant that he was not alone in this place. There were other beings here who could think and hunt and make weapons.

Mark considered his options. Maybe it would be safer to avoid them and move deeper into the dark jungle. They would never find him there. But what about the blue light? He couldn't stop searching for it. It was the only link to home and his mother and father.

Spontaneously his mind conjured up smells from the bar-becue his dad had cooked in their backyard the day before Mark left to go on his hike. He remembered how comical his father had looked in the chef's hat, which kept sliding down over his ears. The way his mother had kept stealing glances at Mark told him she was worried. She had pretended to be happy, but he could tell.

All that seemed like a hundred years ago. What would they think if they could see him now, ragged and dirty, with thick, tough calluses on the bottoms of his feet? His mother would be shocked. Now he behaved and thought more like an animal than a human, sneaking around the forest. Doing his best to survive.

Willie climbed down from the top branches and sat beside him. Mark stroked the monkey-bear's soft white fur. "What should I do, boy? For all I know, these people, if they are people, could be a worse threat than the Howling Thing."

Still holding the arrow, Mark reached for his homemade bow and climbed down from the tree. He wouldn't think about them now. If nothing else, he had a new weapon. He would study the arrow and design more like it.

The first time he tried to shoot it, his string was too loose and the arrow just plopped into the dirt about twenty feet away. The second time, after he had pulled the shoestring taut on the bow, it flew in an arc across the meadow.

He ran after it. *This is so great.* On his trip to the pool that morning he would gather any small rocks he could find to use as tips. Then he'd come back early from his scouting trip and hunt for feathers. He shot the arrow again. This time he hit the bush he was aiming at dead center.

He retrieved the arrow and went back to his tree to pack a small supply of food for his trip. Along with his tree rocks and his sock of edible insects, he took a long strip of lizard jerky. He'd discovered that if he hung the thin pieces of meat over a limb to dry, he could take them with him on his travels and they wouldn't spoil.

Proudly he reached for his spear. Today he would have two weapons.

But what he needed was a quiver to hold his new arrow. He jammed the tree rocks and jerky in his boot so one sock would be free. Then he tore holes, one on each side near the top of the sock, and tied on a long piece of his old bandage as a strap. He placed the arrow gently in the sock and slung the bow and quiver over his shoulder.

As usual he went to the pool first. He looked for rocks but there weren't many, and they were too smooth and round to be used for arrowheads.

He studied the arrow again. The shiny rock used for the tip was different from any in the area. That meant that the owner of his arrow didn't live around here. He must have come to this part of the jungle on a hunting trip from some other part of the planet.

Mark looked at the mountains. Maybe the arrow people came from there. Suddenly he made up his mind. He wanted to find these people or aliens or whatever they were. Anybody would be better than being alone. That day, instead of circling, he would scout in a straight line.

That morning he had been worried about whoever had left the arrow. Now he was curious, almost desperate, to find out more about them.

chapter 11

The day's scouting trip had taken him into strange new territory. The vegetation was still dense but it was more yellow than red and the trees were short and gnarled. The only animal he'd seen all day was deerlike. She was as big as a horse and had short curled horns. Two small spotted fawns were following her. When she saw Mark, she bounded away with her young close behind.

There had been no sign of the arrow people. Discouraged, Mark decided he must be wrong about them living in the mountains. The next day he would try a different direction.

Sitting down under one of the short leafless trees, he cracked open a tree rock. The forest here was dry, barren and ugly. He was glad he lived where he did. He laughed. He was home-proud. Some branches in a tree and he was proud of them.

He drank the brown juice and contemplated the thought. It was possible that he would never be able to find the light. So far he hadn't really made any long-term plans because he considered all this temporary. But what if it wasn't? What if he was destined to live in this primitive world the rest of his life?

A loud yell stopped his thoughts.

Mark jumped to his feet. A voice—the arrow people. He grabbed his weapons and waited.

Nothing.

Why hadn't he been paying attention? He couldn't tell how far away the voice was or which direction to search in.

The yell changed to an agonized scream. Someone was hurt. Mark started running. He raced through the brush toward the sound.

Just when he thought he'd lost the sound, the terrified scream came again. He tore through the forest, jumping over bushes and ducking under limbs.

He was on it almost before he realized it.

By crouching low in the brush he spotted what seemed to be a kind of dog or wolf. It was standing on its back legs and its head reached high into the low branches. The creature had its back to Mark and was clawing at something in the tree.

The Howling Thing. There was no doubt about it. It was huge, on its back legs at least as tall as Mark. The gray fur on its back was coarse and bushy, and long foamy gobs of saliva dripped from its mouth.

Something in the tree—Mark thought it was some kind of monkey—and partially hidden in the leaves was frantically trying to climb higher, but one arm hung limp and one leg was bloody. The Howling Thing was clawing it to death.

Without thinking, Mark took his single arrow and fitted it to his bow. He stepped out of the trees, aimed, drew and released all in one motion.

The shot was as good as he could hope for. It struck the Howling Thing in the center of the back but it wasn't enough. The beast wheeled and came for him.

Mark stumbled backward, reaching for his spear. He wanted to run but his legs felt riveted to the ground.

The Howling Thing covered the space in three jumps and leaped, its weight carrying Mark back and down and slamming him into the ground. *One second,* Mark thought, *my throat will be gone in a second. Everything ended.*

It didn't happen. He pushed out from under the heavy animal.

The Howling Thing was dead.

When it had lunged for him, Mark had instinctively raised the spear. The sharp point had gone through the animal's heart, killing it instantly.

Blood ran down Mark's face. He crawled to his feet, shaking, staring down. The giant mouth was open, exposing ferocious incisor teeth that would have ripped him to pieces. The claws were longer than bear claws, longer than Mark's fingers.

He swallowed again. *Close this time. Really close. If the spear hadn't taken the animal directly in the heart, if the creature had had half a second longer, I would have been dead. . . .*

Mark suddenly remembered the Howling Thing's victim and looked out across the clearing at the small tree.

It was empty.

chapter 12

Mark followed the trail of blood until it disappeared. Then he continued to patiently search for signs. The few tracks he found resembled small human footprints except for the toes, which seemed to be connected. From what he had seen in the tree, with everything blurred and moving, the small being had two arms and legs. The face had been hidden but he remembered seeing long dark hair.

The heavy grass kept him from finding any more tracks and the trail ended abruptly. The wounded quarry of the Howling Thing had vanished.

"That's gratitude for you," Mark grumbled. He made his way back to the clearing. The Howling Thing lay as he had left it.

It took some doing but he finally managed to twist his spear out of the body. The arrow was another matter. It was wedged next to the backbone, and when he yanked on it, the tip broke off inside the creature.

He studied the dead animal. It was incredible that he had

survived the attack. The thing was huge and built to destroy whatever it pleased. A killing machine.

Yet he had killed it.

An elation filled him. A surge of something he could not define—a strange feeling of power. His chin went up. *I saved a life today and didn't die. I'll make more arrows, better ones. And because of what I have, all the creatures in the forest will be afraid of me.* He jumped to his feet and punched his fists in the air. He wanted to sing, to show what he had done, to tell of it.

"I am the killer of the ferocious Howling Thing," he chanted, stomping his feet in the dirt. "I—am—the— best. I—am—the—killer—of—the—terrible—Howling— Thing."

He took his knife and sliced the long claws off all four of the animal's paws and began whooping and dancing around the bloody carcass until he ran out of breath.

He would take the skin. He could use it for moccasins, a quiver, maybe clothing. He knelt and worked a full hour, peeling a rectangle of hide—about four feet by three—that took in the back and the sides, leaving the skin on the legs, head and feet.

With the skin gone the meat was exposed, and for the first time Mark thought of eating it. It seemed so doglike; the thought of eating dog was not particularly appetizing. But he'd been eating bugs and worms and lizards and the meat looked solid and dark. He cut strips to take back to camp to dry later.

Everything he had been through had made him even hungrier. When he found his supplies, he opened a tree rock and drank the juice while he chewed on strips of lizard jerky.

This place was not going to get the best of him. And if it was true that he might never find his way home, then he would make it anyway. He would become a better hunter and tracker and his weapons would be the best he could make.

Sooner or later he would locate the arrow people. But even if he couldn't find them he would be all right.

He had killed the Howling Thing.

chapter 13

One tree rock after another slammed into his back.

"Stop it, Willie. I don't want to play catch right now. Can't you see I have work to do?" Mark had studied the way the feathers had been inserted into the carved slits in the broken arrow's shaft and copied it. He had found straight wood—a kind of cross between willow and cane—near the clear pool and he used that for shafts.

He still had no rocks for the tips so instead he had sharpened the ends of the shafts into needle points.

There had been no scouting for four days. Mark had been too busy collecting bird feathers and finding just the right pieces of wood to form into arrows. When he wasn't making them he was practicing shooting.

In the evenings, after scavenging for food, he had painstakingly put together a vine necklace made with the claws of the Howling Thing. He never took it off. The meat had been stringy and tough, but not bad tasting, and he'd roasted it on a stick and eaten it until his stomach bulged. He was still hungry in some way. Full, but still preoccupied with food, and he thought of bringing down one of the buffalo beasts.

Willie waddled over and crawled into his lap. Mark put down the arrow he was working on. "All right. Maybe I have enough—for now. I guess I have been kind of ignoring you lately. Come on. Let's me and you take a walk up to the pool."

Mark patted his shoulder. This signal meant the monkey-bear was to climb up on his back. Willie's long furry arms clung to Mark's neck.

Leaving the dark jungle always made the little guy nervous, and the only way he would agree to go was if Mark carried him.

At the pool they stopped for a cool drink. Mark stared at himself in the water. He was so different. His hair hung down to his shoulders and his weapons and necklace made him look like an ancient warrior.

The chunky kid who had begged to hike across the missile range hadn't really been in very good shape. But this kid, the one who stared up at him from the pool, was lean and tough. His forearms were thick and solid, corded with muscle. Now he could climb straight up any of the vines into the tops of the highest trees and even hang by one arm while he collected tree rocks. His senses were tuned and he was becoming a good hunter. The previous night's dinner was proof of that. He'd had his first taste of roasted screaming bird, taken with an arrow high in one of the trees.

Mark watched Willie playing in the water on the other side of the pool. "How about going on a short scouting trip with me, boy? We won't go far. I'll have you back by supper, promise." He patted his shoulder and Willie ambled around the spring and easily jumped up on Mark's back.

Mark walked for more than three miles in a direction he'd never had a chance to try before. The trees began to thin out and the hazy yellow sky was clearly visible. He had become so accustomed to the shade of the jungle that he had to squint to protect his eyes.

The grass only grew in patches here, and for the first time he could see large areas of ground. It was a lot like the dirt on Earth and he guessed that all planets were pretty much the same. What was it Carl Sagan had said? Oh yeah, we're all made out of star stuff—carbons and acids and stone and gas. Dirt was dirt, whatever the planet.

He let it run through his fingers. The next day he would scout longer. Take his bow and quiver of arrows and spear and see what lay beyond the forest. Maybe take Willie with him for company. See how this planet worked.

chapter 14

"*Come on. I said I'd carry you. What's* your problem?" Mark folded his arms and scowled at the monkey-bear in the tree house. Willie had climbed to the top branches and refused to be coaxed down.

"You are such a baby. Okay, fine." Mark picked up his weapons and food stores. "But don't say I didn't offer. You won't see me for a couple of days."

Willie clicked and screamed and shook the branch hard.

"What's with you? Do you know something about that part of the forest I don't?"

The monkey-bear continued to shake the tree and make irritating noises.

Mark shrugged. "If you're worried about me, don't be. I killed the Howling Thing, remember? So just hold down the fort and I'll be back." He turned and walked across the meadow. Willie's clicking followed him until he was out of sight.

Heading in the same general direction he had taken the day before, Mark hurried through the forest. When he reached the thinning trees he slowed. There was not as much cover here and he would be a target for some enemy, like a buffalo creature.

He walked until late in the afternoon without stopping. For reasons he couldn't explain he was extremely anxious to see what lay beyond the trees.

But food was a necessity. Finally he stopped to eat. He wanted to sit in the warm dirt and enjoy the feel of it on his skin, but he knew better. It wasn't wise to stay out in the open. Instead he chose a spot in the shadow of a tree and ate a quick snack of a tree rock and a piece of jerky made from the meat of the Howling Thing.

A new sound came from overhead. Mark craned his neck and searched the leaves. A great bird with a round head like an owl was scolding him for using its tree.

Mark's eyes narrowed. The feathers. They were the same red and black as the ones in the first arrow. The one made by the arrow people. Perhaps the people were close.

He started out again. Walking was easy. The tangled bushes and underbrush had gradually disappeared, taken over almost completely by red sand.

Dozens of large rabbit creatures similar to the one in his meadow jumped out ahead of him. They hopped on their hind legs like kangaroos and scurried into holes near the tree roots in the sand. Mark made a mental note of the new food source.

By dark he was wishing he had worked harder to figure out a way to carry water. The juice in the tree rocks was good but he had been moving quickly and had worked up a powerful thirst for pure water. He would just have to wait.

The day had ended before Mark was ready. He had hoped

to find the edge of the forest by nightfall but the trees, though sparse now, seemed to go on forever. Unless it rained or he found water, he would have to go back the next day. Food wasn't a problem. He could hunt, and he'd almost perfected starting a fire by hitting the back of his pocket knife against a rock he carried in his pocket. If he had the right tinder, sparks would fly into the dry leaves and start them blazing.

After smoothing the sand under one of the scrawny trees, he lay down and rested on his elbows. He chuckled, remembering when building a fire with matches had been difficult and without matches impossible. His father had taken him camping several years ago and they wound up spending the night huddled in cold sleeping bags because they had somehow let their matches get wet.

Thinking of his dad made him feel guilty. It had been five days since he had tried to locate the blue light. He shrugged it off. Making the arrows was important. Eating was important. Living was important. His parents would understand.

It was strange to be able to see the sky at night. Near the dark jungle the only thing you could see when you looked up was trees. The black was overpowering here and he realized that he missed seeing stars.

He lay back and stared into the darkness. Maybe the stars were up there but the ugly yellow haze was just hiding them.

He closed his eyes and imagined stars.

chapter 15

It was early morning. They moved within twenty yards of where he was lying. His eyes were open but he lay absolutely still, not wanting to give away his position.

There were five of them, uncovered from the waist up and obviously females. They were dressed in skins and their black hair hung long and loose. They were carrying large pots and made no effort to be quiet. One of them laughed loudly at something another said.

People, he thought. *Planet people. Not so very different from Earth people.*

When they were safely past, Mark moved to his feet, gathered his supplies and followed them carefully.

They took a well-beaten path, which he probably would have missed if he'd given up and turned back that day. Mark darted from one tree to the next, trying to remain hidden. Soon a vaguely familiar sound reached his ears.

Water. They walked to a small creek that wound its way through the sand and trees. Mark crept as close as he dared and watched.

The girls had dark, olive-colored skin and small eyes with an extra fold of skin on the lids. They spoke a strange clicking language. One walked with a limp and didn't carry a pot. She knelt to drink from the trickling creek and Mark could see the soles of her feet. They had a thick padding, and all her toes were joined by a weblike covering.

When the pots were filled and the girls ready to go, Mark silently moved off the path. They passed right in front of him. Compared to him they were small, standing only about as high as the middle of his chest.

The girl with the limp was last. He got a good look at her injured leg. She had been severely wounded and the torn flesh was just beginning to heal.

Mark's eyes widened. The wound looked as if she had been raked . . . with claws. She had to be the one in the tree when he had killed the Howling Thing. He wanted to step out and call to her but was afraid he might startle them, so he held back.

He trailed them through the scraggly trees and sand into another dense stand of forest. It would have been hard to track them in these woods, but someone had gone to a lot of trouble to hack out a wide path.

The girls stopped to give their injured companion a chance to rest. She sat down on a stump in the middle of the path and waved them on. When they wouldn't go, she said something sharp in the clicking language and waved again. This time they picked up their pots and moved down the trail.

Mark chewed his lip. He had to talk to this girl, but how? She wouldn't understand him.

He waited, watching her, hoping to discover a clue. She

was pretty in a strange way. Her skin was flawless, and except for her small eyes and flat, turned-up nose she looked a lot like people from Earth.

Mark made his decision. Quietly he slipped out of the cover of the trees and stood on the trail in front of her.

She jumped to her feet, her eyes wide with fright. *"Mawof. Ta Ta Mawof."* The girl was poised to run.

Mark stepped back. "I won't hurt you. See." He set down his weapons and held up his hands. "I want to be your friend."

Her terrified eyes went to the claw necklace. *"Kakon ne wat te!"*

"That's right." Mark touched the long claws. "I saved you. I killed the Howling Thing."

Down the trail they heard someone calling. *"Lee-ta? Wak ta to ek?"*

"Is that your name?" Mark asked. "Leeta?"

The girl stared at him. She had relaxed but still looked scared and confused. *"Na to nuk. Na to nuk."* She pointed into the forest, edged around him and hurried down the trail.

Mark hesitated. What should he do now? The girl had pointed into the trees. Why? What was she trying to tell him? He picked up his things. The trees could wait. Right now he wanted to see where Leeta and her friends were headed.

There was no danger of losing them. The trail was wider than most of the bike paths back home. He let them get far ahead and then started off. This area reminded him of his jungle except it had more colors. The plants and trees were not as red and the flowers had tinges of white, yellow and orange.

Eventually sounds of voices and movement came from just beyond the trees. Mark crept closer, lay on his stomach and watched in amazement. Before him, in a large clearing, was an entire village of huts made of sticks. Most were small and round except for the long one in the middle. Some women were roasting meat over an open pit and others were using sharp sticks to dig in a garden. Several children were running in and out, playing a game with a rock attached to a long vine. The men were carving with primitive stone tools or sitting around the fire smoking.

It was like a scene out of prehistoric times. The arrow people wore the skins of animals Mark didn't recognize. There was nothing modern here, no metal tools or cooking utensils. Everything came from their surroundings and was fashioned by their own hands.

The girls took the water pots inside one of the huts. Leeta stayed outside and kept glancing nervously back toward the forest. An older woman spoke to her and she reluctantly went into the hut.

Mark waited a long time but Leeta didn't come out. Hunger gnawed at his stomach. He crawled back into the dense brush and sat on his heels. Now that he knew where the arrow people were he could come back anytime. And because the girls had shown him where the water was, he could stay in this area indefinitely.

First he would eat. Then he would plan how to meet the arrow people.

chapter 16

The water from the creek tasted good, even better than the pool water. In the sandy forest he had made a good shot at one of the rabbit creatures and now he was preparing to roast it over a small fire.

He had decided the smartest thing to do would be to wait in the trees near the spot where he had confronted Leeta. Maybe she would be curious enough to come back and look for him.

A twig snapped behind him. He reached for his spear and turned. There was nothing.

Mark frowned. His ears must be playing tricks on him. Cautiously he stepped behind the fire and waited. There was no other sound, no movement.

After a few moments he went back to his cooking. The green limb he was using as a skewer worked well enough, but he had to be careful not to get too close to the flame when he turned it.

The juices from the sizzling meat dripped into the fire and made a wonderful smell. He quit turning the meat and reached behind him for a tree rock.

His boot was gone.

"What the . . ." Mark looked all around the fire. He could swear he'd had it a few minutes before.

He turned the rabbit meat one more time and took it off the fire. Then he picked up his spear and walked down the trail a few yards. His stomach grumbled, so he decided to go ahead and eat and search for his boot later.

But when he got back to his fire the rabbit was gone. So were his bow and arrows.

Leeta. She'd pointed in this direction and caused him to come here. It had to be her. Angrily he stomped out to the footpath. "Leeta! I know you're out there. Leeta? Bring my stuff back."

A tree rock dropped on his head. He looked up. There she was, sitting calmly on one of the branches, going through his things.

Mark rubbed his head. "That's not funny." He jumped and made a grab for her and she climbed higher.

"Don't make me come up there." Mark started to climb. The strange girl dropped everything except the bow and quiver. She quickly inserted an arrow, pulled it tight and pointed it right between his eyes.

"Now hold on." Mark put his hands in the air. "You've got everything backwards. You're the thief here. I just want my stuff back."

Her chin went up. *"Tso tso Kakon ne."*

"What does that mean? Can I at least get my dinner? I'm starving." He edged toward the rabbit, which had landed a few feet away in a clump of grass.

"Nah. Nah." She shook her head and motioned for him to move away.

Mark stopped. "Look, this is stupid. If you're hungry"— he rubbed his stomach—"I'll give you some." He pointed at the rabbit meat and then at her.

She studied him a long moment and lowered the bow a few inches. Mark grabbed the rabbit, brushed off the grass and walked back to the fire.

He pretended he wasn't interested in her, added some sticks to the fire and finished roasting the rabbit.

She was quick. Even with her injured leg she was able to climb out of the tree almost before he could blink. But she wouldn't come any closer.

He continued to cook, and when the rabbit was done he tore off a piece and offered it to her. She only stared.

"Suit yourself." Mark took out his knife and opened one of the tree rocks. She watched in fascination. He held out half to her. It looked as if she might take it but then she stepped back.

Mark stuffed himself, wiped his hands on his pants and thought about what to do next.

Leeta seemed nervous. She kept looking over her shoulder. Mark was afraid she was about to leave. Jabbing his chest with his finger, he said, "Mark." Then he pointed at her. "Leeta." He went through it again. "Mark . . . Leeta."

It didn't seem to faze her. He tried a different tactic. This time he touched the claw necklace, growled, picked up his spear and stabbed the air.

A small giggle escaped her lips.

He put the spear down. "So you think I'm funny? Well, at least that's something." He sat back on his heels. "Okay. You talk to me."

She continued to stare at him with bright, shiny black

eyes. Behind her there was movement. Mark jumped up, but before he could reach for his spear he was surrounded.

Leeta's tribesmen had their weapons trained on him. Mark glanced around. He had named them wrong. They were the arrow people all right, but they also had clubs, blowguns and primitive crossbows.

A fierce-looking man with black dots tattooed across his forehead and a long, thin bone through his nose stepped in front of the fire. He looked angrily at Leeta. Then he raised his club.

It was the last thing Mark saw before he blacked out.

chapter 17

His forehead hurt and his arm was swol-
len and sore from the sting of the blow dart. Mark held his
head and sat up. He was sitting on a dirt floor inside a round
hut.

Whispers followed by peals of laughter came from the
open door. Mark turned. Several small children were watching him.

He stood up and hit his head on the ceiling. The children
howled with laughter.

"You guys are kind of short, aren't you?" Mark looked
around the small room and spotted his gear lying near the
wall. It was all there, his boot, compass, knife, spear, and
bow and arrows.

He scratched his head. None of this made sense. If he was
a prisoner, why would they let him keep his weapons?

An old woman with short gray hair and a stooped back
entered carrying a large red leaf and a carved wooden bowl
with a glob of steaming white mush in it. She put it down in
front of him and knelt. *"Kakon ke ity."*

Mark looked at the mush. "You want me to eat that?" He raised his hand and mimed putting something in his mouth.

The old woman nodded enthusiastically. *"Kakon ke ity."*

He squatted on his heels and picked up the leaf. "You wouldn't try to poison me, would you?"

The woman gave him a wrinkled smile, revealing that all her front teeth were missing.

Mark scooped up a small portion of the mush with a piece of leaf and tasted it. It was bland but not awful. He took another bite. The woman and children continued to stare at him. Self-conscious, he hurriedly ate the rest, wiped his mouth and handed the woman the bowl. "My compliments to the chef."

She smiled again and backed out of the hut.

Mark followed her to the door. There was no guard. The children were the only ones paying any attention to him. Everyone else was busy with their daily routine.

He stepped outside. No one seemed to care. The youngsters circled him, poking his light skin and pointing at his strange toes and eyes. One little boy touched the bottom of Mark's faded blue jeans. An older child said something in the clicking language and pointed at the claw necklace. This impressed the others and they lined up to get a better look.

"You guys are lucky I don't charge admission." Mark sidestepped them and walked across the open compound.

Two men who were busy decorating a rectangular shield with black and orange dye gave him a friendly nod.

Mark nodded back. "Hi there. Nice day."

They looked at each other, shrugged and went back to what they were doing.

As he walked through the village everyone acknowledged him politely and no one made any effort to stop him.

The fierce-looking man with the tattoo and the bone through his nose was sitting beside a small fire watching him. He gestured for Mark to come over and join him.

The man took a long pull on the slender plant stalk he was smoking and then handed it to Mark.

Mark studied it. The smoldering thing was tightly wrapped with leaves and tied with vines. "My parents aren't going to like this," he muttered. He accepted the foul-smelling thing and took a short, polite puff. The aroma was so strong it made his eyes water. He coughed and handed it back.

The man laughed and slapped Mark on the back. *"Kakon et tu bet."*

"Kakon?" Mark cocked his head. "You people keep using that word." He put his hand on his chest. "Are you calling me Kakon?"

The man slapped him harder. "Kakon."

"Okay, sure. Kakon." Mark sat in silence, watching the activities around him. The women seemed to be working a lot harder than the men. He spotted Leeta in the garden with a digging stick and waved to her. She looked away and kept hoeing.

Mark turned to the man beside him. "Are you the leader of these people? You know, the head? The one in charge?"

The man exploded with a barrage of words. His lecture lasted for several minutes and Mark couldn't understand any of it.

When the man was finished Mark drew a picture in the sand with his finger of several small stick men. Above them he drew a larger figure holding a club. Mark pointed at the figure and then at the man. "Is this you?"

There was another stream of words and then the man jumped to his feet and hurried into one of the huts. In a few seconds he came out and handed Mark his club.

"No, you don't understand. I don't want your weapon. I was just . . ." Mark looked into the chief's eyes. He was staring at Mark expectantly as if he was waiting for something in return.

"You've got this whole thing wrong. See, I really don't have much to trade. Why don't you just keep it?"

The chief continued to wait.

Reluctantly Mark stood and walked to the hut where he had left his things. He studied his small pile of belongings. The problem was, he really needed everything he had.

The compass. He didn't need that. Maybe it would be enough. He came out holding the broken instrument in his outstretched hand. At first the little man just stared at the shiny object. Then Mark jiggled it and the silver arrow in the middle changed directions.

"Ahhh! So so Kakon!" The leader's eyes opened wide. He reached for the compass, holding it gently in his palm as if it was very precious. Excitedly he called to the other men. "Tsik ma Kakon."

The others crowded around and exclaimed over the treasure. Some good-naturedly hit Mark on the shoulder, apparently complimenting him on the trade.

"It's no big deal." Mark shifted. "It was broken anyway." He caught Leeta's eye and moved toward the garden.

One of the younger men immediately stepped in front of him. "Nah. Yi tsi su Lee-ta. Nah."

"Look, pal, I just want to talk to her. She and I are old friends." Mark tried to move around him. The man quickly blocked his way and shoved him.

Mark stood almost a head taller than the young man and he thought about pushing back. He glanced around. Everyone in camp had stopped what they were doing to watch.

Leeta quit digging and gave Mark a stern look.

Mark figured he must be breaking one of their customs. He stepped back. "Okay, okay. I don't want to offend anybody on my first day in town."

The young man's face broke into a good-natured smile. *"Gott Kakon nee."* He took Mark's arm and led him back to the men.

Mark sat with them until it was almost dark, watching them shape and hone their weapons, smoke and talk. Mostly talk. They discussed something nonstop for more than an hour. Mark couldn't understand a word.

At dark the whole village lined up and moved into the long thatch-roofed hut in the center of the compound. The chief invited Mark inside and indicated where he was to sit.

There was a fire in the middle of the windowless room and the people sat in a wide circle around it, watching the smoke curl out a hole in the roof. The chief clapped his hands and one of the men began pounding on a skin-covered wooden drum that made a dull sound like a bongo.

Another man stood up and started moving in rhythm. Mark could tell he was supposed to be a bird flying in the air. The dancer was graceful and quick. He swooped down, as if capturing something on the ground, and "flew" off again.

When he was finished the chief took over and talked for a long time. The children must have heard the speech before because they became restless and went to the back of the hut to play games.

"Kakon tsir tu tu se. Kakon."

Mark jumped when he heard his new name. The chief was motioning for him to stand.

"Me?" Mark's eyebrows went up.

The chief pulled him to his feet and touched the long claws around his neck. *"Kakon tsir nto tu."*

"Oh, I get it. You want to know about the Howling Thing. Okay . . . let's see. Well, it's like this. One day I was out scouting and I was just about to have lunch when I . . ." Mark looked at their faces. The people were staring blankly.

He scratched his head. "I know. I'll do like the bird man and act it out for you. Like I did for Leeta."

At the mention of her name the group turned to look at her. Embarrassed, she covered her face. Everyone laughed.

"Here goes." Mark picked up his new club and started walking slowly around the circle as if he was hunting. He stopped suddenly and held his hand to his ear. Then he crouched low and ran through the crowd until he came to Leeta. He put the club down, dropped to all fours and started growling and clawing at her. She giggled and tried to push him away.

Stepping back a few feet, he pretended to shoot an arrow at the Howling Thing. Then he reached for the club and readied himself for the beast to attack.

Here he decided it would be more impressive to alter the story a little. Instead of falling down when the Howling

Thing rushed him, he stood his ground and stabbed the make-believe monster until it was dead. Then he put one foot on its head and raised his pretend spear in victory.

The people all started talking at once. Apparently he was a hit. Mark bowed and sat down.

The chief patted Mark on the head, then clapped his hands again, and the villagers stood and filtered out of the room, each one patting the top of Mark's head as they walked by.

Mark didn't know what he was supposed to do.

Leeta hung back. When they were all gone she pointed at him. "Mawk." Then she indicated herself. "Lee-ta."

"Yes! Oh yes!" Mark grinned. He held out the weapon in his hand. "Club."

"*Ksaa.*"

He jumped up and ran to the middle of the room. "Fire."

She followed. *"Tisa."*

"We're talking." Mark grabbed her shoulders. "Can you believe it? Leeta and Mark are talking."

Leeta smiled shyly. "Taw-kin."

chapter 18

Since no one told him any different, Mark decided to spend the night in the same hut where his belongings were stored. There were several other young men already lying on the dirt floor when he entered. Without complaining they moved and made room for him.

Mark lay down but he couldn't sleep. So much had happened that it was hard to take it all in. One thing he knew: It felt good to be around other people. Especially these people. They were so innocent and friendly.

He assumed Leeta must have come to his defense earlier when they had captured him. He couldn't wait to talk to her again. Maybe she knew something about the blue light.

As usual when he thought of the light, it brought back memories of what life had been like before. He'd been here a long time. Almost a year or maybe more.

Sleep finally came. But it felt as if he had just closed his eyes when the others in the hut began stirring. Someone was shaking him.

He opened one eye. It was the same young man who had

prevented him from talking to Leeta in the garden the day before. *"Kakon gut no ma."*

Mark crawled to his feet and followed the men outside. The women were already up. They had the fires going and were serving bowls of the hot mush.

There was no talking. The men ate quickly and gathered their weapons.

Mark finished his food and went to collect his spear and bow and arrows. If they were going on a hunting trip he didn't want to be left out.

Leeta touched his shoulder. She had a worried look on her face. *"Mawk. Se dtsik nah. Nah."* She shook her head.

"What? You don't want me to go? Sorry, I have to. I can learn a lot from these guys. Besides, I don't want them to think I'm a sissy or something."

Leeta stomped her foot. *"Nah. Mawk. Nah."*

Mark folded his arms. "Yes, Leeta. Yes."

She made an angry face and marched to the young man who had awakened him. They argued in a whisper for several minutes. Then she dragged him over to Mark. *"Mawk. Tukha."*

Mark nodded at the man. "Tukha."

The young man seemed upset about something. He motioned for Mark to come with him. The two of them took their place at the end of the line and followed the rest of the men out of the village.

Once they were in the forest, the group moved into a trot. Occasionally a couple of the men would break off from the rest, then meet them farther down the trail.

Mark would have liked time to study the new terrain but every time he slowed, Tukha urged him to keep up.

About noon the group stopped to rest and eat. Mark was amazed at the number of birds they cooked. Somehow, the two men who had kept leaving the group had managed to shoot enough along the way for every member to have plenty of food.

They were allowed one drink from a skin bag containing water and then they were on their way again. Tukha always stayed at the end of the line with Mark.

It was obvious they weren't hunting for small game because they passed up several good opportunities to kill rabbit creatures. Mark decided they must be after something big.

At dusk the men gathered around the chief, who held out a small skin pouch containing a tarlike substance. Each put his fingers in and smeared some of the mixture on his face.

When Tukha was finished with his own face he decorated Mark's. The tribe looked different now. More fierce and warlike.

They walked silently through the forest for another half hour until they came to a sandy clearing.

Mark couldn't believe his eyes. It was another small village. He was excited. So there were other people on this planet. Some of them were bound to know about the light. Someday, when they understood each other better, maybe he could get Leeta to come with him and talk to them about it.

The men spread out and hid in the bushes until long after the sun went down. Then the chief raised his club. They stormed out of the trees and raced down into the village yelling and screaming.

Mark started to join them but Tukha grabbed his arm

roughly. *"Kakon nah. Tsid Lee-ta. Sek tu."* Mark wasn't quite sure what he said except that he didn't seem to want him to go and it had something to do with Leeta.

Tukha pointed at the bushes, indicating where Mark was to stay. He raised his club threateningly. *"Sek tu."*

"Okay. I'm not stupid. I can tell when I'm not wanted." Mark sat down in the sand.

When Tukha was sure Mark wasn't going to follow him, he turned and ran into the village after the others.

Still not sure exactly what they were up to, Mark moved to his knees so that he could see what was going on.

The scene in front of him was chaos. The arrow people were setting fire to the huts and running through the compound overturning cooking pots and smashing things.

Mark was stunned. He didn't understand. These were supposed to be the good guys. The same friendly peaceful people who had practically adopted him the day before were now doing everything they could to destroy this village and the people in it.

The men in the huts were taken by surprise but they soon came out fighting. The arrow people were ready. They fought one on one and drove the villagers back into the forest. Women and children ran screaming for their lives. The fire had reached almost every hut and now it lit up the whole area like a giant bonfire.

To his right, Mark saw Tukha fighting. Tukha tripped and went down. His spear flew out of his hand and one of the villagers began beating him senseless with a heavy club.

Mark jumped out of the bushes. "Stop. You're killing him."

The little man was frightened out of his wits when he saw

the tall, light-skinned boy come charging out of the forest. He stumbled backward and ran off in the opposite direction.

Mark dropped his club, grabbed Tukha's arms and dragged him back into the brush. He shook the young warrior but Tukha's eyes didn't open.

The other arrow people were coming back now. They were ecstatic because they had managed to chase off most of the villagers and steal everything of value that hadn't been smashed to pieces.

The chief raised his hand and was about to give the signal to withdraw when he spotted Mark trying to revive Tukha. He shouted orders and two of the men hurriedly picked up the young man and carried him ahead of the others into the forest toward home.

chapter 19

Tukha was dead.

The village had suspended work and spent the entire day preparing for his last rites. Mark stood in the shadows watching the funeral procession. Six men carried the lifeless body to a raised wooden platform that was decorated with flowers, vines and leaves. They placed him on top along with his spear and shield.

Tukha's family, which consisted of his sister—who turned out to be Leeta—and an older woman, walked slowly to the beat of the drum, then covered Tukha's face with an animal skin.

Someone handed the chief a burning torch and he touched it to a small stack of firewood underneath the platform. Everyone stepped back to watch the body burn.

Mark had made up his mind. He couldn't stay with these people. They were too different. They had wiped out a whole village as if it was a huge game. In the morning he would go back to his tree house and live alone in the dark jungle.

He felt a hand on his shoulder. Leeta had brought the old woman to him. Her sad eyes searched his face. *"Kakon es tat mek Tukha."* Tears ran down her wrinkled cheeks.

"I'm sorry," Mark said. A lump welled up in his throat. "Your grandson seemed like a good man."

Leeta led her grandmother away and when the fire had completely consumed the body the people crowded into the long hut to talk about the raid, divide the booty and console the family.

Mark didn't go. He wished it wasn't so late. If he could, he would leave right now. None of this made any sense. The arrow people hadn't really gained that much from looting the village, just a few new weapons, some beads and a small amount of food. Nothing they brought back seemed worth dying over.

He went into the hut where he'd slept the night before and picked up his things. The hiking boot still contained one tree rock, a couple of pieces of jerky, an empty sock and a few strips of cloth. He had replaced the shoestring with a vine and now he tied the boot to his belt loop. At first light he would be ready to go.

"Mawk?" Leeta stood in the door.

Mark didn't look up. He grabbed his spear and bow and arrows and brushed past her. His intention was to spend the night at the edge of the clearing and start back first thing in the morning. He would forget these people and their crazy customs and concentrate on finding the blue light.

Leeta followed him past the huts. He stopped and looked at her. "Where do you think you're going?"

"Lee-ta, Mawk, taw-kin?"

"There's nothing to talk about. Go back to your crazy

people before they catch you out here and decide to kill me too."

Leeta untied a string of wooden beads from around her neck and put them in his hand. She gave him a sad, confused look and turned to go.

"Wait." Mark caught her arm. He took off his broken watch and fastened it around her tiny wrist. "Thanks for everything, Leeta. Maybe I'll see you around sometime."

She stroked the watch. *"Et tkus Kakon Mawk."*

"Yeah, same to you." He put the beads in his boot and walked to the edge of the clearing. When he reached the trees he glanced back over his shoulder.

She was gone.

chapter 20

The air smelled like smoke. It was still dark, too early for the women to be cooking. Mark's eyes snapped open. There was a heavy, dark cloud hanging over the village. He crawled through the brush to get a better look.

The meeting hut was on fire.

His first thought was that the other tribe had come after them looking for revenge. But when he saw the attackers he knew he was wrong.

These warriors were not simple village people. They rode large long-haired creatures that looked like a cross between a horse and a cow, and their weapons were made of metal.

The arrow people didn't have a chance. Those who tried to fight were cut down immediately. Mark saw the chief and several of the men die fighting with primitive clubs against swords and axes.

Some tried to run. They were chased and either stabbed by the mounted men or trampled by the mounts.

Mark scanned the grounds, frantically searching for Leeta. He ran into the clearing, calling her name. A wild scream came from the garden area. One of the men had her cornered and was bearing down on her with his mount.

"No!" Mark started for her. A rope settled around his neck and dragged him back. He hit the ground hard. The rope was choking him. He fought and grabbed at it with both hands but it was no use.

The man pulled Mark on his back through the sand to the center of the village clearing, where the invaders had rounded up several of the men, women and children.

Mark loosened the rope and threw it off. He stood and saw Leeta being pushed roughly across the compound to join them.

When she spotted Mark she ran to him and held on to his arm. *"Es Tsook. Tsook."*

The men surrounded them. They were much larger than the arrow people and their skin was a light yellow, but they had the same odd eyes.

The leader, a fat man wearing a long cape made of hides, gave a command and the warriors dismounted and began tying the arrow people together.

Mark found himself at the front of the line with Leeta tied securely to his right wrist. He could see that the Tsook, as Leeta called them, had not come to plunder the village for goods. They were after people. And now he was one of their prisoners.

The fat man was staring at him. Mark stared back. The man's eyes narrowed and he yelled an order in a new language. One of the warriors put the rope back around Mark's neck and held the other end in his hand as he climbed onto his beast.

The leader gave the command and the men rode out of the village, dragging Mark and what was left of the arrow people along behind them.

part

2

chapter 21

It was feeding time. As usual the Tsook tossed a leftover hindquarter of raw meat in the dirt and scarcely waited until it was gone before they gave the order to move out again.

The routine had been the same since the terrible day they had been captured. Tied together, the prisoners trudged along behind the riders all morning, and then in the afternoon the column stopped for a short break to eat and drink.

Their numbers had dwindled from twenty-five to twelve. The Tsook did not tolerate weakness. Any of the captives who fell sick or lagged behind was immediately killed.

Leeta gnawed on a piece of the raw meat. She noticed Mark watching her and held it out to him. "Mawk eat."

Mark shook his head. He and Leeta were getting better at communicating. They spoke an odd combination of the clicking language and English. He'd learned that the name she had called him frantically when he had first confronted her, Mawof, was a mythical creature the old people used to scare the little ones into behaving. His new name, Kakon, was more difficult for her to explain. She could only tell him that a *kon* was a very important warrior. And *ka* meant the second or younger one.

When he questioned her about the blue light, she claimed to know nothing. But Mark noticed that every time he brought it up, she seemed nervous and eager to change the subject.

He was also picking up a few phrases from the Tsook. Their language was easier than Leeta's because he could hear distinct vowels. He understood when the leader, Dagon, gave orders to stop and go, or for his men to feed the prisoners or take care of the mounts.

Mark swallowed dryly as he watched Leeta and the others gobble up the raw meat. It wasn't that he wouldn't eat it. He often did when he couldn't find insects or edible plants along the trail. Sometimes he took a small portion just to keep himself from starving. But it rankled him to be treated this way and by now he was used to going without food. When he had broken his ribs he had conditioned himself to eat only when it was absolutely necessary. So it wasn't hard to let the others have the meat.

Dagon always watched Mark carefully. At feeding time he would stand near him, staring openly as if he was inspecting a novelty in a sideshow. It made Mark feel uneasy, though he understood he was different from the arrow people and that his skin was lighter and he was taller than the Tsook. Even his clothes were unusual. He'd outgrown his jeans and was now wearing pieces of them he'd wrapped around himself.

Once, Dagon pointed to the hiking boot Mark kept tied to his belt and used the word *Merkon*.

"Not Merkon," Mark said flatly. "I am called Kakon."

Dagon's second in command, a surly bearded man called Sarbo, angrily drew his sword and threatened to drive it into Mark's chest for daring to speak to the leader. Dagon stopped him.

That had been more than a week before. Now they were resting at the foot of the very mountains Mark had promised himself to visit someday. He only wished he had come here under different circumstances.

Dagon was studying him again. Mark ignored the man and turned to Leeta. "How long till we reach the land of the Tsook?"

Leeta glanced up at the mountain. "Go over." She held up three fingers. *"Tkas."*

"Three days?" Mark chewed his lip. "Then what?"

"Nah kirst ma." She held up a wrist that was tied with rope. "Tsook war to take workers."

"I noticed your people weren't exactly against making war."

Leeta shrugged and took another bite. "Way much people."

Dagon gave the order to break camp. The arrow people quickly stood and formed a straight line. The men no longer put a rope around Mark's neck. Either they thought it would be too hard for him to escape while tied to the others or they knew he would never be able to outrun their animals.

The thought of escape had crossed Mark's mind more than once. The Tsook had not bothered to check the contents of his boot, so he still had his pocketknife, which would easily cut through the rope. But so far he hadn't had a good chance to use it. By day the Tsook watched them carefully and at night a guard was posted.

As they climbed higher up the mountain the terrain became rocky and the air difficult to breathe. The arrow people were used to flat, humid land and they were having a hard time keeping up with the animals.

Leeta cried out and Mark felt an abrupt tug on the rope. He glanced back. Leeta had stepped on a sharp rock and sliced the bottom of her foot.

The riders immediately closed ranks. Leeta bit her lip, looked straight ahead and kept moving.

Mark could see blood on the side of her foot. "Is it bad?" he whispered.

"Bad, yes."

Mark slowed the pace as much as he dared. Soon Leeta was hobbling and the line was barely moving.

Sarbo stepped off his mount and drew his sword. Mark knew what was about to happen. The Tsook would kill her, throw her body to the side and go on without a second thought.

The yellow-skinned man moved to the front of the line. He cut the ropes that connected Leeta to Mark and the person behind her.

Leeta closed her eyes.

"Stop!" Mark yelled in Tsook. He stepped between her and the man.

The executioner's eyes flashed. With his free hand he shoved Mark out of the way and raised the sword.

Mark gathered himself and charged. He rammed the warrior with his shoulder, knocking him off balance.

Surprised, Sarbo stumbled and turned on him, swinging the heavy sword in a wide arc. Mark dropped to the ground and the death blow missed him by inches. He rolled to the side and sprang to his feet, waiting for Sarbo's next move.

"*Ho yat Sarbo,*" Dagon commanded the warrior.

Sarbo hesitated, his sword still raised. He gave Mark a contemptuous look, spat at his feet and swaggered back to his mount.

Mark looked up into Dagon's eyes. They were like cold, black stones. He couldn't read any emotion. Why this man continued to spare his life was a mystery.

Dagon ordered Mark back to the line.

Mark hurried to Leeta and looked at her injured foot. The gash was deep, slicing through the clear thin web between two of her toes. Without waiting to see what the men would do, he took the roll of cloth from his boot, gently wrapped the wound and slipped one of his threadbare socks over it. Then he told her to climb up on his back.

A tear slipped down Leeta's cheek. She nodded gratefully and threw her arms around his neck. Mark shifted her weight and took his place in line.

They moved on.

chapter 22

*That night they camped in a small clear-*ing on a tree-studded ridge. The Tsook were running low on food and water so the prisoners had to do without.

The men were restless and their tempers were constantly on edge. Sarbo tried unsuccessfully to pick fights with several of the warriors. Mark did his best to stay out of the big man's way.

He understood enough Tsook to know that they were almost at the end of their journey, two more days at best. As he rewrapped Leeta's foot he tried not to think about what that would mean.

"There. That ought to do it." Mark had ripped the insole out of his boot and used it as a cushion for the bottom of her foot. "Does that feel any better?"

She didn't answer.

He glanced up. The way she was looking at him made him uncomfortable. She had an odd smile on her face, as if she knew something he didn't.

Confused, he scratched the back of his neck. "I . . . guess we'll be at the Tsook village tomorrow."

Leeta nodded. She gently stroked the broken watch he had given her and kept smiling at him.

"Uh, well, it's late . . . *ksee tu*. Better sleep now." Mark scooted down on his back and closed his eyes. The last thing he needed was for Leeta to start acting weird on him.

The Tsook had left him untied. He turned over. If ever he had a good chance to escape, this was it. The men were tired and quarrelsome. And they were so close to home they probably wouldn't even bother hunting him.

On his own he would be able to move faster. He could make it down the mountain in less than a day and then cut cross-country and head straight for the dark jungle.

The dark jungle. Willie had probably given up on him and gone back to live with the other monkey-bears by now. And of course there was the blue light. It was out there somewhere. He had to start looking for it again.

There was no way to be certain, but he estimated that he had been in this world for well over a year. Perhaps even two years. That would make him close to fifteen years old. Had his parents come to terms with his disappearance? Were they getting on with their lives? He sighed, then shifted and opened his eyes. Leeta was still sitting beside him, caressing the watch. He frowned. What would the Tsook do to her if he left?

"You go?" she asked.

How did she know? It was almost as if she could read his mind. Mark stirred uneasily.

He closed his eyes again. "Go to sleep, Leeta."

chapter 23

Mark set Leeta down and let her walk for a while. They were on a well-traveled road in the bottom of a beautiful red valley. The crimson grass was knee high and there were fruit trees and fields of bright orange flowers on either side.

The odor of manure and roasting meat wafted down the path toward them. From behind some rocks on the hillside came a long clear note from a hunting horn. It was answered by another horn farther down the valley.

A churning cloud of dust sped down the road toward the caravan. The animal that reined up in front of them was a golden color with a well-brushed coat. The rider was a girl with long black braids who was dressed in buckskins like the warriors. She wore beautiful tanned-leather moccasins that reached past her knees.

Dagon jumped off his mount and ran to greet her. He gave her a bear hug and swung her around. When he put her down she glanced back at the captives. Her eyes fell on Mark. She stared openly the way her father had done.

"Megaan . . . Kakon," Dagon said in a low voice.

The girl raised her chin haughtily, turned back to her father and smiled. She said something Mark couldn't make out, then climbed back on her mount and rode next to Dagon to lead the procession into the village.

From the outskirts Mark could see that the Tsook were far ahead of the arrow people in building design and construction. This was more than a small village, it was a bustling town. Their houses were made of logs that had been fitted together and chinked with mud. And they had high lookout towers at every corner so that they could easily spot approaching enemies in time to warn the people.

The manure smell had come from the large wooden pens a few hundred yards in front of the buildings. They contained a small herd of tame buffalo creatures.

A cheer went up as the warriors came closer. The Tsook people stood outside their houses and clapped and yelled as the group passed by.

The prisoners were led through the maze of fires, cooking pots and houses to the far side of town. The ropes that had held them together were removed and the warriors began pushing the prisoners over the edge of a deep pit.

Mark looked down. It was at least an eight-foot drop. One of the warriors shoved him forward. He shook the man's hand off and glanced across the pit. Dagon was on the other side watching him. Mark set his jaw, stepped out and landed on the bottom with the others.

The arrow people were frightened and huddled together in the middle of the pit. A crowd of Tsook villagers gathered around the top and pointed and stared at the prisoners.

Mark found a corner and sat down. He was tired and his

back ached from carrying Leeta. Yawning, he put his hands behind his head and leaned against the dirt wall. He knew he had done the right thing by staying. Leeta never would have made it without him. But it didn't make what was happening now any more pleasant.

Leeta knelt beside him. "Mawk tkan tu."

"You don't have to thank me. Anybody would have done the same."

Above them some sort of trading was going on. Voices were raised and there was arguing. Mark figured the Tsook were trying to decide how they were going to divide the slaves. It didn't concern him. As soon as he had rested he would be gone. And they wouldn't be able to catch him either. His plan was to move fast and stay in the brushy country where the mounted men couldn't go.

The arguing and trading lasted for hours. Finally, late in the afternoon, everything was settled. Suitable terms had been reached and the new owners came for their property.

One by one the captives were hauled out of the pit and handed over to their Tsook masters. When it was Leeta's turn she held on to Mark's arm and had to be pried loose. The elderly woman who had purchased her prodded her with a sharp stick, forcing her to move away.

Mark was the only prisoner left in the pit. The crowd had thinned out and the warriors were dividing up the payment.

Apparently no one wanted him as a slave. That was just as well. Because in the morning they would have realized what a bad trade they'd made when they found him missing.

"Kakon." A sharp voice called to him from above.

He opened one eye. The girl with the long black braids was standing over him with her arms folded. She barked an order, and a rope circled his head and settled around his shoulders. Sarbo jerked Mark to his feet, and some of the warriors helped pull him out of the pit onto his stomach. One of them held him down while another quickly tied his hands together.

Sarbo got up on his mount and barely gave Mark time to stand before he dragged him through the village to a small outbuilding behind one of the larger log houses.

He shoved Mark inside the shed and bolted the door. The smell was awful, like an open sewer. It would have been pitch black in the tiny room except for a small semicircular opening near the bottom of the back wall. Mark crawled through the slime on the floor and looked through the hole.

There were fat, hairy piglike animals with long, pointed snouts rooting in a pen attached to the back of his cell. No wonder it smelled so bad. He was in some kind of pigsty.

He moved to the door and tried it. It wouldn't budge. He pushed on the walls. They were solid, made of logs like the houses. That left the opening. He knelt by it again. It was so small he doubted he could get his head through, much less his body.

The floor. It was dirt. He would dig his way out. But first he had to get his hands loose. Feeling in the bottom of his boot, he found his knife and began to saw awkwardly on the rope. Minutes later it snapped off his wrists.

He dug at the base of the opening, using everything he could find—his knife, the toe of his boot, his fingers—until finally he had a hole big enough to fit his shoulders through. He wriggled into the pen.

He hadn't really planned to escape until it was dark but he couldn't take the chance they might discover the hole.

Staying low behind the log fence, he crossed through the herd of pigs and peeked up over the side of the pen. There was no one in sight.

It was now or never. He took a deep breath and slid over the fence. He moved carefully from one building to the next until he had made his way to the edge of town.

Ducking behind some tall red plants in a garden, he took a quick look around. The road they had come in on was to his right. But taking it was out of the question. They would catch him if he stayed in the open. He looked to the mountains. They were steep and rocky but would have better places to hide.

Mark crawled along the rows of vegetables. There was only one more house to get past and then he would head for the rocks and brush on the hillside.

He raced to the back of the building and leaned against it to rest. The move nearly cost him his life.

A small furry animal—he hesitated to call it a dog but it had some of the same features—started up a scrawking sound. Mark knew there was no time to lose. He bolted for the closest ridge. Behind him he could hear shouting and the sounds of people running.

Something whizzed past his ear. An arrow hit the dirt in front of him. He dodged to the left and zigzagged up the mountain. He was nearly to the top of the ridge. If he could just make it to the brush they'd never catch him.

He felt something slam into his back. It ripped through his flesh like a hot iron. He fell to his knees. Twice he tried to get up but couldn't. He clawed at the ground, then managed to get to his knees and pull himself behind an outcropping of rocks.

The voices were getting closer. Mark fought for air. Something was taking his breath away. With his last spark of consciousness, he felt around for something to use to defend himself. His fingers closed around a large rock. He tried to pick it up but he was too weak; it fell from his hand.

Then they were on him.

chapter 24

The heavy steel band around his ankle dug into his skin as he walked. The chain forged to the band held a heavy iron bar that made his movements slow and clumsy.

It had taken almost three months for him to heal from the arrow wound. And the moment he had been well enough to sit up, Dagon had had the village blacksmith build the ankle chain.

Dagon's daughter, Megaan, had tended to him personally. She and her grandmother had removed the arrow and treated the deep laceration. And all the time he was healing she taught him the Tsook language, which he now spoke almost like a native.

He had been given an old pair of buckskin pants to wear and was allowed to sleep on the floor in a corner of the house. Dagon had issued orders that Mark was to be fed generous portions. He said he wanted him fully recovered so that he could do the hard work he had been purchased for.

Mark hadn't seen Leeta since the day she had been

brought in and sold. And he was too proud to ask Megaan about her. He could only hope she was being treated well.

"Kakon. Pay attention. I need your help with this." Megaan scowled at him and pointed to the buffalo hide they were dipping into a foul-smelling liquid to tan it. "I think if you don't stop dreaming all the time I will have to tell my father how useless you are."

"And I think I would be far more useful if I had this chain off my leg and wasn't forced to do women's work."

Megaan raised an eyebrow. "You would run."

"I might." Mark helped her lift the heavy, wet hide. "I told you I have to get back to the dark jungle and look for the blue light."

"I'm not sure I believe you about this. Probably it is a wild story that you have concocted to fool us."

"Then how do you explain why I look so different? Have you ever seen anyone else in your world who looked like me?"

"Transall. I told you before, the Tsook word for the world is *Transall*."

"You didn't answer my question."

"I think this one is finished. Help me hang it over the fence. We will work on it some more tomorrow."

It was always the same. Megaan avoided talking about the blue light and the possibility of his returning home.

She brushed the hair out of her eyes. "Now we will go to Tanta's storehouse. We are almost out of pole flour."

Mark stared at her. "We? I am to come with you? I thought your father said—"

"My father said that I am in charge while he is away. And I need you to come with me to carry the sacks. Get the cart."

Megaan's grandmother appeared at the door of the house. "Do you think it wise to take the savage manboy among the real people? He might embarrass you."

The old woman always called him the savage. Many times Mark had heard her go on and on about how the Tsook were the original people. They were specially made by the Creator of Life to rule Transall. Everyone else had been provided to serve the Tsook and to be used however the people wished.

"What can he do?" Megaan asked. "Besides, I need pole flour and Barow is too small to help me carry it."

"I am not too small." A little boy with curly black hair was standing near the door. He stuck his head outside and pouted. "I am a brave warrior like my father, the great Dagon."

Megaan smiled indulgently. "Someday, my little Barow. Someday."

"Take one of the field hands," the old woman said sharply. "They can move about more easily than this one. I've never understood what your father sees in this giant savage. Why in the name of Transall does he let him stay in the house and feed him good Tsook food like a pet? He should sleep in the fields with the others."

"I have made my decision." Megaan watched Mark pushing the small two-wheeled cart toward them. "If he misbehaves I will have him whipped. He knows this."

Mark brought the cart to the front of the house and waited for instructions. He towered over Megaan and they both knew that the only thing that kept him in the village was the heavy iron shackle clamped around his leg. He did what he was told in order to get along. For whatever reason,

Dagon treated him better than most of the other slaves, and Mark wanted no trouble until he could find a way to escape.

He followed Megaan down the narrow path leading from her house to the central road through the large village. So far he'd never been allowed to leave Dagon's property. His chores consisted of feeding the stock, working in the house garden, chopping wood and carrying water to the field hands and herders. The main section of town had been off-limits until now.

It was hard for him to keep up with her. Not only did he have to push the unwieldy wooden cart but he had to cope with the iron bar on its short chain as it dragged along behind him.

They passed several women sitting outside their houses sewing. Megaan waved and called each of them by name. Mark felt them staring at him as if he had two heads.

Not only was he unusually tall, with strange disfigured eyes and feet, but he was a slave who had tried to escape and yet was allowed to live. This was a feat unheard of among the Tsook.

The village was presently inhabited mainly by women and children. Dagon had taken most of the men out on a raid. Only those thought essential to keep things running smoothly had been left: the blacksmith and the slave over-seers with their deadly crossbows. A few elderly men sat around doing nothing but chewing a smelly kind of tobacco.

Mark had overheard Dagon planning his next attack with Sarbo and some others. Across the high mountains to the east lived a group of savage people known as the Rawhaz, cannibals who had slaughtered a party of Tsook from another village. Dagon and his warriors had joined forces with them and gone out to find and destroy the man-eaters.

Mark had been waiting for a time like this to make a run for it. With the warriors gone there would be no one to come after him. But first he had to find some way to get rid of the chain and bar.

He heard the clanging sound of metal hitting metal and stopped to stare at the fiery forge in the blacksmith's lean-to. Fire. If he had a tool and could get the chain hot enough . . .

"Kakon. Must I always yell to get your attention?"

"Huh? What did you say?" Mark rolled the cart up to Megaan.

"I said . . . Oh, what is the use? You will never make a good worker. I do not know what ever possessed my father to think that you and the Merkon could possibly . . ." Megaan's eyes widened and her hand went to her mouth. "What I meant to say was that you should quit dawdling."

That was the second time Mark had heard that name. Why was it such a secret? He tried to walk faster.

"So who is this Merkon, anyway?"

"Here is the storehouse. You wait outside while I go in and barter with Tanta." Megaan walked to the large building without looking back.

Mark sat on the ground. Megaan infuriated him. She always had her nose in the air and never answered any of his questions. One of these days . . .

"Mawk." Mark heard a familiar voice calling to him from across the street. It was Leeta. She was walking behind an old woman and carrying two heavy baskets.

"Leeta." Mark jumped up. "How are you? Are they treating you all right? *Ksee tyaak tu?*"

The old woman glared at him. "No talking, slave. It is not permitted." She poked Leeta with a stick and they moved on down the road. Leeta looked back but didn't say anything.

Mark watched to see which house she went into. It was a square one with a thatched roof at the end of the street.

"Kakon. What are you staring at? Quit gawking at that stupid slave girl and come get these sacks." Megaan stood in the door of the warehouse, frowning. "My grandmother was right. She said you would embarrass me."

Mark turned slowly. His jaw tightened and he spoke carelessly. "Leeta is smart. You will not speak of her like that."

Color flooded Megaan's cheeks. "I told you to come and get the sacks. Don't make me tell you again."

chapter 25

"A windmill? What's that?" Barow pushed the door open so that Mark could carry in the heavy wooden buckets of water.

"It's a wind-powered machine that can bring water up out of the ground."

"What sort of nonsense are you filling his head with now?" Megaan knelt by the fire, stirring the stew in a large hanging pot.

"It isn't nonsense." Mark set the buckets on the table. "Where I come from no one carries water. It is piped right into your house and when you want some all you have to do is turn a handle and out it comes."

Megaan laughed. "And I suppose you can have your choice of boiled or freezing cold?"

"As a matter of fact, you can."

"What will you come up with next? This morning you told him that your people are able to fly above the clouds inside metal birds." Megaan handed Mark a bowl of hot stew. "This is quite a magical place you come from."

"Don't make fun of him, Megaan." Barow pointed at the claw necklace around Mark's neck. "He is a brave warrior and he knows many things. What about the drawings he made in the dirt? Did you ever see such wonderful things— tall buildings, carts on four wheels that go by themselves, and a box with changing pictures? If it wasn't true, Kakon would not say it was."

Mark ruffled the little boy's hair. "I'm glad someone around here believes me."

"Hrummp," said Grandmother. "Megaan, why do you let Barow trail around after that savage? Nothing but trouble will come from it."

Megaan turned. "Kakon is harmless, Grandmother."

"Harmless? I've seen him eyeing your father's old crossbow above the fireplace. One night we'll all be killed in our sleep."

"Speaking of sleep . . ." Megaan yawned and wiped her hands. "It's time we all turned in. They will be bringing in the harvest tomorrow. There will be more work than we can handle. Come, Barow."

Barow leaned close to Mark. "Someday, when I am chief, I will order her around." He stood and followed his sister and grandmother into the sleeping room.

Mark gulped down the rest of the stew. He moved to his mat to wait. It was almost too easy. Megaan and her family were used to hearing him move around at night. No one considered the possibility of his escape, because he was hampered by the leg iron.

He let hours pass before he moved to the fireplace and reached for Dagon's old crossbow and quiver of arrows.

He stooped to pick up the bar and slipped quietly out the

door. A dog howled in the distance, reminding him of what had happened the last time he'd tried to escape.

At the woodpile he grabbed the short ax and hurried behind the house and through the garden. He headed across the fields. Dagon's overseer had taken the field hands to work down the valley for the big harvest, and there would be no one to hinder him.

Steadily Mark made his way to the top of the first hill. He stopped and looked back, thinking of Leeta. If he went back for her they would both be caught and this time Dagon might not be so generous. There was nothing Mark could do. He would just have to go on alone.

After the first ridge he picked up the pace, scrambling through the trees and brush as fast as he dared in the darkness. By morning he would be so far away that they'd never find him.

chapter 26

It was early. The sun wasn't quite up and Mark's footsteps were dragging. The only time he had stopped during the night was in a secluded valley, where he'd built a small fire to heat the metal chain. When he had it hot enough he used the ax and pounded at it until one of the links broke.

After that he had kept moving, afraid to stop for fear someone in the house had discovered that he was missing and sent out a search party.

True to his plan, he stayed in the worst possible terrain. The brush and rocks would make it harder for the riders to come that way. But he was still anxious. The Tsook knew the area better than he did. They might know a way to circle around and get ahead of him.

Mark moved down a shadowy gorge, looking for an out-of-the-way place to hide and rest for a while. A noise ahead stopped him.

Someone or something was coming his way.

He scrambled up the side of the hill and hid behind some

trees. His heart pounded in his ears. Surely the Tsook hadn't caught up with him this soon.

In seconds a party emerged from the shadows. They were small men with streaks of blue and black paint on their faces and chests. Their heads were shaved except for one patch of long hair in the back. The only clothing they wore was a breechcloth hanging from a piece of leather around their waists.

They carried blowguns and spears. A few had swords, axes and bows like the Tsook. Mark counted thirty-seven of the small men as they passed silently in front of him.

It didn't take a genius to figure out who they were. Around their necks the men wore bones and shrunken skulls. Scalps with long black hair decorated their weapons. These were the Rawhaz whom Dagon and his men were looking for.

And they were headed toward the Tsook village.

Mark was torn. With the warriors gone, the villagers were in terrible danger. And Leeta was back there. He thought of little Barow, who followed him around and hung on his every word. Even Megaan with her superior ways didn't deserve to be dinner for the Rawhaz.

He had to go back. As soon as the Rawhaz were out of sight, he came out of hiding. There was only one way to beat them to the village and even then it would be close. He had to take an open route and use the road.

Either way it was dangerous. If the cannibals didn't find him and he managed to get to the village first, the Tsook would probably kill him before he had a chance to explain why he had come back.

Mark's tiredness disappeared and was replaced by a frantic urgency. He sprinted up one hill and down the next, stopping only a few times to catch his breath and grab a drink from a mountain stream.

It was midafternoon when he reached the red valley and the road that led to the village. He jogged past the buffalo pens. The scouts spotted him and gave a single blast on the horn.

"Rawhaz!" Mark sputtered. His throat was so dry he could barely get the word out.

The blacksmith and two warriors who had stayed behind were standing in the road waiting for him.

One of the warriors grabbed him. "What is the leader's slave doing carrying a weapon and running loose among the people? Has Dagon's daughter gone mad to allow this?"

Mark swallowed. This was incredible. These men hadn't been out looking for him. They didn't even seem to know he was missing. Megaan must not have reported it.

The warrior shook him. "Speak up, fool. Have you nothing to say for yourself?"

"Yes." Mark gasped for breath. "The Rawhaz . . . are . . . coming."

The blacksmith stepped back. "How do you know this thing?"

"I . . . saw . . . hurry . . . they can't . . . be far."

"Go back to your master's home, slave. I will sound the alarm. But be warned. If this is some kind of trick . . ."

"No . . . trick. I saw . . . with my own eyes."

The warrior let Mark go, shoving him in the direction of Dagon's house. Mark stumbled and continued down the lane.

Megaan was standing outside the cabin working on a

hide when she saw him. She glared at him. "So you have come back. Did you forget to take something else that was not yours or were you just too much of a coward to keep going?"

Mark half fell against the cabin wall. He waited until he could speak clearly. "I didn't have to come back."

"Then why did you?" Megaan spat the words at him.

"The village . . . I ran into some Rawhaz headed this way."

The tower guard blew the alarm.

Megaan hesitated, but only for a second. "Come this way, Kakon. We must get Barow and my grandmother to safety. There is a cave down the valley in the white rocks not far from here."

"You go on ahead. I'll catch up with you. I have something to do first."

"The slave girl?"

Mark nodded.

Megaan touched his arm. "The cave is hidden. Look for a dead tree with its roots exposed." She turned and ran into the house.

Mark hurried back through town. People were running everywhere. Some were leaving the village, pushing carts and carrying their belongings on their backs. Others were preparing to fight.

He pounded on the door of the square, thatch-roofed house. The old woman opened it a few inches. "What do you want? I have no time for you. Go back to your master."

Mark shoved the door open, knocking the woman back. "Where is Leeta?"

"You insolent dog!" the woman screamed. "I will see you whipped for this."

Leeta stepped into the room. "Mawk. Run away. Now is time. Go-hurry. Go-hurry."

"Not without you." Mark took her hand. He looked at the old woman. "You can come with us. I know about a hiding place."

"I would rather die."

"So be it. Come, Leeta. There's not much time."

The street was still in turmoil. There was another long blast on the horn. The warrior who had stopped Mark on the road earlier galloped his mount to them. "Can you ride, boy?"

"A little. Why?"

"What you said was true. Our scouts have located the Rawhaz. All our men are needed to fight. We need you to ride for Dagon or the village will be lost."

Leeta grabbed his arm. "No, Mawk. No do this. Please no."

Mark sighed. "Leeta, go down the valley. Look for a dead tree in front of white rocks. A cave is there. Tell Megaan I sent you. Go on. Do what I say. Later I'll come for you."

Leeta bit her lip and moved away.

The warrior slid to the ground. "Take my animal. You'll find Dagon somewhere to the east in the badlands. The Rawhaz will not attack until nightfall. I think we can hold them off . . . for a while."

Mark pulled his exhausted body up on top of the beast. The animal shied sideways and he held on with both hands.

The warrior caught the bridle and handed Mark a hunting horn. "Blow this and Dagon will come to you. Now hurry." He slapped the animal's haunches with the flat part of his sword and it lunged into a dead run.

By the time Mark gained control of the animal and could look back the warrior was already out of sight.

chapter **27**

The creature beneath him was larger and more powerful than any of the horses Mark had ridden on his uncle's farm. Every step the muscular animal took seemed to ripple through its entire body.

And this was the first time Mark had ever ridden without a saddle. The thin blanket stretched across the wide back of the animal wasn't made for comfort.

Mark let the beast choose the direction, hoping it would take him to one of Dagon's familiar campsites. He'd never been on this side of the mountain and had no idea where to look for the Tsook leader.

When he was safely away from the village he blew the horn. There was no answer.

The countryside here was different from what he had seen so far of Transall. This area was bleak and lifeless. The trees had thinned out and the cracked ground was an ugly gray sand.

He rode for miles across the parched open land, blowing the horn now and then and listening for a return call. But the only living things he saw were some long spotted lizards and a few big ugly birds that resembled vultures or turkeys.

It dawned on him that he hadn't eaten anything for a long while. He thought about trying his luck with Dagon's crossbow but knew there was no time. He nudged the animal with his heels. Night was falling and the Rawhaz would begin their attack soon.

Mark's eyelids grew heavy. "Wake up," he told himself. "There are people back there counting on you." He blew on the horn until his lips hurt from the effort.

The animal kept moving, its hooves tapping out a steady rhythm. Mark laid his head on the shaggy animal's thick neck and knotted one hand in the long, tangled mane. The giant beast plodded on, unaware that its rider had fallen fast asleep.

Mark dreamed of the elusive blue light. It was right in front of him. But every time he got close it moved just out of his reach. He chased it but it never stayed in one place long enough for him to catch it.

Then something felt different. The animal had stopped. Mark sat up, wiping at his eyes. The sun was up and they were far away from the mountains. He had slept through the night. He grabbed the horn from around his neck and blew.

On the horizon he could see a band of five or six riders approaching at a gallop. He sighed with relief. Dagon or some of his warriors had finally heard him and were on their way. The village might still have a chance.

Mark pulled his mount to a stop and waved. The animal seemed nervous. It stamped the ground and refused to stand still.

"What's the matter with you?" Mark squinted into the

distance. The beasts pounding toward him were Tsook, all right. But the riders weren't. They were much smaller. More like the . . . Rawhaz.

Mark whipped around, dug his heels into the animal's sides and jerked it into a lumbering run. There was no cover here. Nowhere to hide. Mark exploded across the desert, blaring out notes on the horn as he went.

Twice he glanced over his shoulder. They were gaining on him. If he didn't shake them soon, they would catch him.

To his right was a small barren bluff. He changed direction and headed for it. In front of the bluff were dozens of small rodent holes. Mark saw them, but not soon enough. His beast stepped into one, stumbled and went down.

Mark flew over the animal's head and slammed against the hard ground. The impact knocked the wind out of his lungs. Gasping for breath, he crawled to his feet. The animal was still down, moaning softly, its front leg jutting out at a sharp angle.

A cloud of gray dust boiled toward him. The Rawhaz had changed direction too. In minutes they would be on him.

Mark examined the crossbow. It was still intact. He grabbed the quiver of arrows, scrambled to the other side of the fallen beast and lay down on his stomach. Taking the arrows out of the pouch, he inserted one in the bow and placed the rest within easy reach.

The beast rocked back and forth, trying to get up, grunting in pain. Mark stroked its back. "Just lie still—it won't be long now."

The Rawhaz were just yards away now. Mark took aim at the closest rider and let go. The arrow struck the little man in the shoulder and he twisted and slid off his mount.

Quickly Mark reloaded and fired again. This time his aim was off and the arrow ripped into a beast's chest. The animal fell, rolling head over heels and crushing its rider.

The men kept coming. Mark fired and missed. Arrows and darts landed all around him. One pierced the neck of his mount and the creature stopped moving.

Mark raised himself up to shoot again and narrowly missed being kicked in the head by a giant hoof as one of the Rawhaz jumped over him. Mark flipped around and sent an arrow flying into the man's back.

Pain shot through Mark's leg. He looked down. The tip of a spear had grazed the fleshy part of his thigh. Blood was oozing out.

The two remaining Rawhaz had dismounted and were slowly circling around his dead beast.

Weakly Mark reloaded. He knew he couldn't get them both, but one cannibal was definitely going down.

He lay still, his breathing low and even, waiting for them to come.

Someone shouted. He heard footsteps running away. Mark pulled himself up to see what was happening. The two Rawhaz were trying desperately to catch their mounts.

In front of him, the Tsook were charging toward them. Dagon and his men raced across the desert, firing a volley of arrows as they came. The Rawhaz fell before they could mount.

Dagon slid to a stop and noted the bodies scattered about. He rode around Mark's beast to see who had done all the fighting. His eyes widened. "Kakon? What in the name of Transall . . ."

Mark took a ragged breath. "There's no time to explain. I

was sent to find you. The village is in danger. Another band of Rawhaz is attacking them. You've got to hurry. It may already be too late."

"Sarbo, bring up one of the Rawhaz mounts for Kakon." Dagon turned to Mark. "Is your wound bad? Are you able to ride?"

"I think so. But don't wait for me. You must go."

Dagon dropped his water pouch and supply bag in the dust beside Mark. "Here, Kakon. When you are able, come back to the village. We have much to talk about." He gave the command and the warriors moved out at a run.

chapter **28**

It was a warm day and the bodies of the dead Rawhaz and beasts were beginning to stink. Mark was lying against the belly of his slain beast, taking advantage of what little shade it offered. He had cleansed his wound and cut the riding blanket into strips to wrap it. In the supply bag he'd found several pieces of jerky and a crusty piece of bread that satisfied his hunger.

The animal Sarbo had caught for him stood patiently at his feet. It was time. Mark's leg was stiff and burned like fire but it was time. He collected the water bag and his weapons and supplies and forced himself to stand.

It was bad, he told himself, but he'd had worse when he was shot in the back. Taking the bridle, he led the large animal alongside his dead beast. Then he climbed on top of the carcass, swung one leg over the new animal and started out.

Holding the beast to a walk, Mark made his way back toward the mountains. It was slow going but by the end of the day he reached the first line of trees. He let the animal keep walking until it was almost too dark to see. Finally he slid off, tied the beast to a tree and fell asleep on a pile of dead leaves.

The next morning he awoke in the same position in which he'd fallen asleep. As a result, his leg was even more sore and stiff than it had been the day before.

Gingerly he pulled himself up and rested his back against a tree. The supply bag still had a few pieces of jerky and there was a swallow or two of water to wash it down. He finished the food and was about to try to stand when he heard someone calling for him.

"Kakon? Do you hear me? It is Megaan. Please answer."

Mark remembered the horn that was still around his neck. He blew on it and in minutes a golden beast crashed through the trees.

"There you are." Megaan jumped down and ran to him. "My father said you were wounded. I brought a poultice and bandages."

"The village?" Mark asked. "Is it all right?"

Megaan dropped to her knees and cut away a large piece of his skin pants so that she could work on the wound. "Parts of it are burned, the storehouse has been destroyed and some of the people are dead. But my father and his warriors arrived in time to save the rest."

"Leeta?" Mark squirmed when Megaan applied the medicine. "How is she?"

"Your friend is well. She found the cave and hid with my family until it was over."

"Did Dagon send you after me?" Mark asked.

Megaan frowned. "Just lie quietly until I finish, and stop wiggling like a baby every time I touch you."

"He doesn't know you have come, does he? I think he would be very upset if he knew you were this far from home with all the fighting that's been going on lately."

"My father knows I can take care of myself. He does not tell me what to do."

"If no one sent you, then I guess you must have ridden all this way because you were worried about me. Somehow that doesn't sound right. What's the matter? No one left to do the chores for you?"

Megaan stood. "I am finished. We can go now."

"Is that an order?"

She looked away. "I no longer give you orders. My father says you are . . . Never mind. Can you stand?"

"That depends. What does your father say I am?"

Megaan rolled her eyes in exasperation. "He told the people that you are very brave and risked your life for us. Because of what you have done, he says you are no longer a nonperson. You are an equal."

"How about that?" Mark rubbed his chin. "And what does it mean—to be an equal? Do I get to come and go as I please?"

"Yes."

Mark looked at her steadily. "Seems like an equal ought to get more than that."

"It means . . . you may have a beast and a plot of land to farm and build a house on, and you may ask for a wife when you decide to marry. Now get up. I don't have all day."

"That sounded an awful lot like an order." He raised himself up. "Could you give me a hand?"

Megaan pulled him to his feet and helped him walk. "I

think that is enough help. Wait here, Kakon. I will lead your mount to this boulder so you can get up more easily."

"What was that bit about asking for a wife?"

Megaan scowled at him. "You are too young for a wife."

"I was just kidding."

"I do not find you funny." She handed him the reins. "Can you get on your animal, or do you want me to do that for you too?"

Mark climbed up on the boulder, gritted his teeth and hopped on. Megaan was already on her beast, heading back through the trees. He trotted up behind her. "Thanks for coming to look for me, Megaan."

"You are welcome. But it was nothing. I would have done it for anyone. Even a nonperson. Besides, I suppose I do owe you for saving our lives."

She kicked her beast into a run and left Mark in the red dust.

chapter **29**

The storehouse and some of the other structures were still smoldering when Megaan and Mark rode in. The tower guard announced their arrival with the horn but most people were too busy rebuilding to pay any attention. A few stopped what they were doing long enough to wave or yell out their gratitude as Mark rode past.

Several beasts were tied outside Dagon's cabin. Megaan helped Mark dismount. "Go into the house, Kakon. I will take care of our mounts."

Mark limped to the door and opened it. Dagon and some men were sitting on long benches at a large wooden table.

"Come in, Kakon. The council and I were just talking about you." Dagon indicated an empty seat. "Sit down and hear how the Tsook reward those who help them."

Mark hobbled to the end of one of the benches. "Megaan has told me that you have made me an equal. I thank you."

"Did she also tell you that as soon as the village is defensible again, we will hold a great feast, inviting all the Tsook of

Transall? When the Overlord, the great Merkon, sends his emissary, then the rites of warriorhood will begin."

"For me? You want me to be a warrior?"

"You have proven yourself worthy."

"Again I thank you, but . . ." Mark looked around the table at the war-hardened faces. How could he tell them that all he really wanted was to be free to search for the light and go home?

He swallowed. "What I mean to say is that you have already given me far too much. The place of warrior should be reserved for the sons of the Tsook."

Dagon pounded the table. "It has been decided. Anyone who disagrees with this will answer to me."

The men of the council stood and filed out of the room. Dagon remained sitting. "You are allowed to choose a plot of land, Kakon. While you are trying to decide, you may live in the house of Hagis. He was a brave warrior who died fighting the Rawhaz. I will send Megaan to make sure it is well supplied. Is there anything else I can do for you?"

Mark looked down at the steel band around his ankle. "Did Megaan tell you the reason why I no longer wear the weight on my foot?"

"She explained that she needed an extra hand in the field that day for the harvest, so she ordered it to be taken off. If I had been here I would have been angry, but as it turned out she made the right decision. Do not worry. I will have Tybor, the blacksmith, remove the rest. There is no need for it now."

Mark stood. He couldn't remember ever being so tired. "I'd like to go to that house now. My leg is starting to bleed again and I must sleep."

"Of course." Dagon went to the door and called for his daughter. Megaan appeared and he gave her instructions.

Outside, Mark untied his mouse-colored beast and led it down the road. "I'm sorry for teasing you earlier, Megaan. It really was kind of you to come help with my wound."

Megaan kept walking.

"Your father gave me an odd explanation of how the iron bar came to be off my leg."

"Would you rather I had told him you were a runaway slave?" Megaan snapped.

"Why didn't you?"

"This is the house." Megaan stopped in front of a one-room cabin. "Hagis was an old bachelor. There is no telling what we will find inside." She pushed open the door and went in.

Mark wrapped the reins around a post and followed her in. She started checking the shelves in the back. "This house is a disgrace. I will send a slave up later to clean it for you."

"No. It will be fine until I can do it myself."

"But—"

"No slave will work for me. Do you understand? It is wrong to force others to do your work."

"Oh, really?" Megaan put her hands on her hips. "And just how do you intend to work your new land, Kakon? Warriors are not farmers."

Mark dropped wearily to the torn sleeping mat on the floor. "I haven't thought that far ahead. But I can tell you one thing. If I can't do it myself, it just won't get done."

"Mawk." Leeta burst through the door. "You all right. I glad."

Mark sat up on his elbows. "This is my new house, Leeta. What do you think?"

"It is good house." Leeta wrinkled her nose. "But I clean."

"What about your owner? She might not like it if you're gone too long."

Leeta smiled and spoke in fluent Tsook. "My new owner is Megaan. She took me in."

"It was nothing," Megaan said. She scowled and moved to the door. "The old woman was killed trying to run from the Rawhaz. With you gone we needed another worker. Leeta will take your place, that is all."

"I swear, Megaan." Mark shook his head. "Why is it so hard for you to take a compliment? Just because you are the chief's daughter doesn't mean you're not allowed to say thank you."

Megaan lifted her chin. "Come, Leeta. Kakon needs his rest."

Leeta followed her out the door and then stepped back in. "I be back, Mawk."

"Do that. And if your boss isn't too busy acting like a snob, bring her too."

The door slammed.

chapter 30

Mark felt better than he had in a long time. The iron band was off his leg and his wound was nearly healed. The past few weeks had been spent learning to ride, hunt with a crossbow and fight hand to hand with a sword.

Sarbo was his chief teacher, and the big man demanded perfection. "Not like that, Kakon. If you strike from above you have more power but your opponent will come in underneath and run you through. Try it again."

Mark removed his sword from the practice dummy, stepped back and wiped the sweat off his forehead. This time he whirled and came in from the side, slicing the dummy in two.

"Better. Much better. That will be enough for today. Go home and eat. Come back tomorrow."

"Wild horses couldn't keep me away."

"Wild horses?"

"It's an expression, Sarbo. It means nothing will stop me from being here."

"Strange boy." Sarbo picked up the dummy. "I will take this to my wife to repair. She will have it ready tomorrow. And Kakon?"

"Yes?"

"I do not think you are ready to take on any of the wild horses—whatever they are. Wait until you are a better rider."

"Right." Mark smiled, put his sword in his belt and started up the road.

Tybor, the blacksmith, shouted at him. "Kakon. Come see. I think I finally have it right."

Mark trotted over to the smoke-filled lean-to. "Let's see."

Tybor reached behind him and brought out a flat piece of lightweight metal. "Well? What do you think?"

"This is it. This will make a perfect breastplate. It's light and it won't weigh me down. What about the helmet?"

"It is a much more difficult problem. I am still working on it."

"Great. Let me know when you get it done." Mark turned and headed up the road to his house.

"Wait for me, Kakon." Barow ran up behind him. "You said you were going to show me more writing today. Did you forget?"

"I didn't forget. Come to my house. I will make us a fine meal and then we can begin."

"I already ate, Kakon. Let us begin now. I've been practicing. Watch." Barow bent over and wrote his name in the dirt.

"That's good, Barow. What else can you do?"

"I can make all the letters. Today you should teach me how to write more names."

"I don't know. You need to work on the sounds some more."

"Will you teach me if I tell you a secret?"

"I might. Depends on the secret."

"Dagon has set the time for the feasting."

"Well?"

"Will you teach me?"

Mark tousled the little boy's curly black hair. "I guess so. Now tell."

"It will be at the new moon. And guess what? A messenger has come with word that the great Merkon will be here in person. It will be a very big event." Barow frowned. "Will you still be my friend after you are a warrior?"

"Why wouldn't I?"

"Megaan says—"

"Megaan doesn't know everything. Here's my house. Do you want to come in and watch me eat or come back later?"

"I have seen the kind of food you cook. I will come back later."

"Hey!" Mark pretended to be angry. "You'd better watch it or I won't make you any more of my special brain pizza."

Barow giggled and ran across the road. "I do not think that would be so great a loss."

Mark opened the door to his cabin. A wonderful smell filled the room. Leeta was kneeling by the fireplace.

"Hello, Mark," she said in Tsook. "I have made bread and stew. Megaan says you are poisoning yourself with your own cooking."

"Megaan is an interfering busybody who needs to learn to mind her own business."

"Do you want me to take the food away?"

"Uh, no. I wouldn't want all your hard work to go to waste."

Leeta filled a bowl and set it on the table. "You and Megaan should not fight all the time. You are both good persons. Why do you not get along?"

"I get along with everybody. It's Megaan who has the problem. She thinks she's in charge of all Transall." Mark tasted some of the hot stew. "This is great, Leeta. You should have some."

She filled his glass with water and sat down across from him. "Are you happy here, Mark?"

"I guess so." Mark shrugged. "It sure beats living in a tree."

"What about the blue light and the world you came from? I remember a time when you would have done anything to get back to it."

Mark wiped his mouth with the back of his hand. "I still want to go back. And I will. It's just that right now the Tsook are really going out of their way for me and I don't want to let them down."

Leeta spit on the dirt floor. "The Tsook are slavers. They are no better than the cannibals who attacked us. Are you forgetting how they brought us here against our will? Don't trust yourself to them, Mark."

"Hold on. You're the one who was just telling me how great Megaan was. She's Tsook."

"As in all groups there are some who are different. Tell me, Mark, can you remember your people? I remember mine and I will never forget what the Tsook did to us."

Mark tried to visualize his parents' faces. Vague images of a slightly balding man and a petite blond woman came to him but that was all. He put his bowl down. It had been so long since he'd seen them he was having a hard time remembering what they looked like.

"I have upset you." Leeta stood. "I am sorry."

"Wait. Don't go. You're right. I have lost sight of what is important. After the feast I will leave here. I don't owe these people anything. You can come too if you want."

"There is something I must tell you, Mark. Once, a shaman, a very powerful medicine man, visited our village. He talked of your light."

"Why haven't you told me about this, Leeta?"

"I was afraid. The shaman said the light held more evil power than we could imagine. He said if we ever saw it we should run away as fast as we could."

"Did he tell you where it was?"

"He said the light does not stay in one place."

"My dream. Leeta, I had a dream about the blue light moving away from me. Did the medicine man tell you anything else?"

Leeta chewed her bottom lip. "He said . . . what came from the light would have the power to destroy our world."

chapter 31

"*What is the matter with you, Kakon? You* do not seem like yourself today." Dagon was putting the finishing touches on a new crossbow. "You have nothing to be anxious about. The feasting begins tonight. And the Merkon's messenger has sent word that the Overlord will arrive tomorrow in time for the games."

"I'm not anxious. I was just thinking." Mark scraped the shaft of an arrow. "Dagon, I've been curious. Who is this Merkon? Does he come from another Tsook tribe?"

"The Merkon is the leader of all Transall. He lives across the great river and is coming many miles to meet you."

"Why would he do that? Why would he travel here to watch my ceremony?"

"The Overlord was invited and chose to come. That is all I know. We have not seen him on this side of the river in years. He always sends an emissary to collect our tribute. It is a great honor that he wishes to visit us in person."

"Maybe he's coming to check up on you, Dagon. You know, make sure you're doing things the way he wants."

"There is no need. We are only a small village on the outskirts of many others that are much larger. And we pay our tribute each year. The Merkon would not waste his time checking on us."

Mark sat back. "Are you telling me there are bigger towns than this one?"

"Of course. The Tsook are more numerous than the stars. Unfortunately, there are also many tribes of nonpersons in Transall. It will take time but we will conquer them all."

"Is this the Merkon's plan?"

"In the time before the Merkon, even the Tsook fought among themselves. The land was constantly at war. Now we are united under his leadership and peace is more common."

"Kakon." Barow stuck his head out the door. "Megaan and Leeta have something they want to show you."

Mark set his arrow on the ground. "What is it?"

"You will not be able to see from there," Megaan shouted. "Come inside."

Mark stepped across the threshold and stopped. The girls were holding up a brand-new set of clothing made of soft off-white leather with long fringe on the sleeves.

"We made them for your ceremony, Mark," Leeta said proudly. "Do you like them?"

"Of course I did all the sewing," Megaan's grandmother said smugly. "These silly girls would never have gotten it right on their own."

Mark touched the new clothes. "I've never had anything so nice. I don't know what to say."

"You could say thank you," Megaan teased. "Unless those words are too hard for an important warrior to say."

"Unlike some people"—he made a face at Megaan—"I can say thank you . . . all."

"You'd better hurry home and get ready." Megaan put the buckskins in his hands and pushed him out the door. "We cannot have you embarrassing us at the feasting."

Dagon grinned at him. "It is a dangerous thing to have women sew for you, Kakon. Next thing you know they will be telling you to take a bath."

"In my case that might not be such a bad idea." Mark picked up his arrow. "Thanks for the carving lesson, Dagon. I'd better do as she says and go get ready."

People waved and called to him as he walked down the road. The same women who had stared scornfully when he was shuffling along in chains now offered him fresh bread. He was living the life of a celebrity and it was tempting to stay here forever.

Leeta had declined his offer to go back to the jungle with him. The few who were left in her tribe were now slaves of the Tsook and she wanted to stay with them. He understood. Family was important. He had lost sight of that once but he wouldn't let it happen again.

The festivities were supposed to last through the night and most of the next day. After that, things would settle down and then he would be on his way. No one would question him and no one would come after him. He was an equal, allowed to go wherever he pleased.

In his cabin Mark heated some water and washed the grime off his body before he put on the new buckskins. They fit perfectly. He put on his claw necklace and tied his long hair back with a piece of leather. Megaan would not be able to find any fault with him tonight, he thought, then wondered at the thought—wondered why he cared. Megaan?

A horn blew and drums started pounding. It was beginning. For some reason he felt nervous. He checked himself over, from his bare feet up to the fringe on his shirt.

The door opened and Sarbo stepped in. "You look very fine, Kakon. The festivities are starting and no one will eat without the guest of honor. Come."

"I was just on my way." Mark followed him out the door and up the street. Near the center of town, tables and benches had been set up and the tables were piled high with food. Torches with bunches of flowers tied to them lined the road.

Dagon motioned for Mark to come to the head table. Sarbo sat beside him and whispered, "They have outdone themselves for you, Kakon. This is far better than any ceremony I have ever seen."

The tower guard blew the alarm. It was quickly followed by one long calming note.

Dagon stood. "Apparently our guests are early. Come, Kakon. We will go to meet them."

Mark followed Sarbo and Dagon to the edge of the village. It was almost dark and hard to make out the faces of the approaching strangers.

Nearly fifteen riders stopped in front of them. They wore a crude armor that reminded Mark of the kind he and Tybor had been working on. The leader wore a lightweight metal headdress that masked the top part of his face. He was unusually tall.

"Welcome," Dagon bellowed. "Welcome to the great

Merkon and his friends. We are honored to have you visit our small village. You are just in time. The feasting is about to begin."

One of the front riders spoke. "The Overlord wishes to see the one you call Kakon."

Mark stepped forward. "I am Kakon."

The man in the mask stared down at him through tiny slits in the metal. No one moved or said anything. Finally the Merkon raised his hand. The front rider got down and held the reins of the Merkon's beast.

The Overlord dismounted and turned to Dagon. "Let the feasting begin."

Sarbo showed the riders where to put their mounts and Dagon led the Merkon to the tables, boasting about Mark's heroic deeds all the way.

When they were seated, the Merkon questioned Mark. "Tell me why. Why would a slave risk his life for the people who captured him?"

Mark answered honestly. "It was not an easy decision. I considered saving only myself. But it didn't seem right to let everyone else die."

"Perhaps you only wished to be rewarded?"

Mark's eyes narrowed. He answered evenly, "Perhaps."

The Overlord smiled and reached for a piece of roasted meat. "I think I like you, Kakon. You are not only brave, you are intelligent. You will make a fine warrior."

Mark wasn't hungry. The Overlord's strange behavior had taken away his appetite. He looked down the table. Megaan was sitting with a group of her friends, laughing and having a good time.

The rest of the Tsook were already caught up in the festivities. The children were playing a game of tag and their laughter filled the night air.

"I think I forgot something back at my cabin," Mark said to Dagon. "I will be right back."

He left quickly before anyone could protest. The party was for him, but strangely he didn't want it. He just wanted to be alone. The Overlord made him feel uncomfortable. Something about the man was all wrong.

The embers of a fire were still glowing in Mark's cabin. He sat on his sleeping mat without bothering to light a candle.

"What's the matter with you?" he whispered to himself. The fire sputtered and a spark shot out on the swept dirt floor.

Mark stared at the ceiling. He knew the answer. The real truth was that he was going to miss this place. It had been the only real home he'd had in more than two years.

The door opened. "Kakon? What are you doing here?" Megaan asked. "The stories have started. You should hear Sarbo. He is telling of the time he single-handedly fought off an entire den of the Woompass devils."

"That sounds like Sarbo. You go on back. I'll be along."

"Are you sick?"

"No. Don't worry about me. I said I would be there."

Megaan stepped closer. "I am not going until you tell me what is wrong."

Mark looked up at her. She had a large red flower in her hair and it was the first time he had ever seen her in a skirt. "You look nice, Megaan. It was good of you to get all dressed up just for me."

"Ha! You are so arrogant. If you were a true Tsook you

would know that it is customary for the chief's daughter to . . ." She stopped. "No, I know what you are up to. You are not going to make me angry tonight no matter what you say."

"What if I told you that I am leaving the village after the ceremony tomorrow?"

Megaan bit her lip. "What do you mean, leaving? You will be coming back, will you not?"

Mark shook his head. "Remember when I told you about the place I came from and the light that brought me to Transall? I have to find that light. As you just said, I am not a true Tsook. My people are waiting for me on a different world. I have no choice but to try to go back."

"You have a choice." Megaan marched to the door. "Go back, then. Take your stupid slave girl with you. I do not care. I am sorry I ever knew you."

Mark watched her stomp out the door and spoke quietly in the darkness. "I think I'm going to miss you too, Megaan."

chapter 32

The evening seemed to wear on forever. Mark returned to the celebration and Barow insisted that he tell the story of the Howling Thing, even though the little boy had already heard it a dozen times.

Dagon told the story of finding Mark pinned down behind his dead beast, loading his last arrow, ready to die for the Tsook. This brought the people to their feet, yelling and praising their young guest of honor.

The Merkon still made Mark feel uncomfortable. Every time Mark looked at the man he found a pair of cold dark eyes inspecting him.

The storytelling and feasting lasted until late. The smaller children had to be carried home and put to bed and some of the men went with them. Other men drank so much they fell asleep at the tables.

Mark found his way back to his cabin and tried to sleep but tossed and turned for hours. It seemed he had just fallen asleep when he awoke with a start.

The Merkon was sitting at his table watching him. "I hope I did not disturb you, Kakon."

"No . . . no." Mark blinked and sat up. "I was just taken by surprise a little, that's all. I am not used to people coming into my house unannounced."

The Merkon's lips went white. His eyes seemed to flash beneath the mask. "You are not afraid of me, are you?"

"Should I be?"

"It might be wise. I could easily order your head sliced off and fed to the beasts of the forests." Two of the Merkon's men stood in the doorway. The Overlord waved them away. "Wait outside."

He turned to Mark. "I understand you are interested in finding a certain light. A light with great power."

Mark stood and walked cautiously around the table. "How do you know this?"

"I make it my business to know everything that goes on in Transall."

"Then you know why I have to find it."

The Merkon tapped the table. "I have been told that something has happened to you to make you believe that you are not from our world and that the light is the way out."

Mark folded his arms. "I do not believe it—I know it."

The Merkon studied him. "Dagon speaks highly of you. For this reason, I have decided to help you. After the ceremony you will travel with me to Trisad. There is an old shaman there. If anyone knows of your light, it will be he."

The Merkon moved to the door, his breastplate clanking and his long cape of skins flowing behind him. "We will leave tomorrow." The tall man pulled the door shut behind him.

Mark dropped to the bench. This put a new twist on things. The Merkon made him feel uneasy. Mark really didn't want to travel anywhere with him and his army of stone-faced bodyguards. But what if this was the same shaman Leeta had told him about? It might be the only real lead he would ever get. He had to go.

His mind was made up. He washed the sleep out of his eyes and stepped outside.

Sarbo was waiting for him, mounted, holding the reins of Mark's gray beast. "Get on, Kakon. Did I not tell you that the race would begin the first thing this morning?"

"You told me. But after last night I didn't think anybody would be too serious about it. Especially you. Didn't I see you fall asleep in your bowl?"

Sarbo stiffened. "I was only resting. If you had not left the feasting when you did, you would have seen that I got my second wind."

"Sure. And what did you do then? Stumble home to your wife?"

"Kakon, if you were older, I would . . ."

Mark laughed. "Then I guess it is a very good thing that I am not."

Sarbo threw the reins at him. "Get on your mount. After I trounce you soundly in this race perhaps you will show a little more respect for your betters."

"What if I win?"

"You? That is a great joke. You hardly know how to sit on a beast."

"Then let's make a wager," Mark said confidently. "If I beat you, you will give me your . . . new sword."

"Ha! And when *I* win, you will give me that necklace you are so proud of."

"Done." Mark swung up on his mount and followed Sarbo down the road.

Mark was surprised to find almost every man in the village on mounts, gathered near the buffalo pens. Even some of the Merkon's men were entering the race.

Dagon climbed a corral fence and stood on the top rail. "You will race up the valley to the large sand blossom tree. There Tybor will be waiting with a basket of pagoma fruit. Place a piece of fruit in your teeth and race back. The first man to pass me still carrying the fruit will be declared the winner."

The villagers lined the beginning of the route. Mark spotted Leeta and Barow waving at him. Megaan wasn't with them.

Dagon continued. "When you hear the horn the race will begin."

The riders moved into position. Mark found himself between a stranger and Sarbo. He turned to his teacher. "Good luck."

"You are the one who needs luck, Kakon. Get ready to lose your precious necklace."

The horn blew and fifty beasts thundered down the valley, leaving the spectators in a cloud of choking red dust.

Sarbo's animal pulled slightly ahead of Mark. Mark held on with both hands and urged his beast to move faster.

The road was a blur. The animals plowed up the ground,

fighting for the lead. A black beast cut in front of Mark and he had to pull up.

Something rammed into his back, knocking him off balance. He grabbed frantically for the mane. His animal kept running and Mark could feel himself slipping. With all his strength he held on, wrapping one arm around the beast's neck.

Inch by inch he lost control, until he went over. His hand was still tangled in the mane when his feet hit the ground, where he flopped around like a rag.

The black animal that had cut him off was now practically on top of him. The rider pulled up beside him, crushing him against his mount's belly before veering off.

Mark's arm felt as if it would rip loose. He called to the beast to stop but the animal only ran faster, its hooves clipping Mark's side with each stride.

Using his free hand, Mark groped for the reins. His fingers found them and he yanked, sawing on them until the animal finally stopped, its sides heaving.

The race was still in progress. Mark clawed his way back onto his beast and kicked it back into action. Riders were passing him on both sides. Ahead he could see the sand blossom tree. Tybor was standing under it hurriedly passing out the pagomas.

Mark slid to a halt and waited for Tybor to get over to him. The smith tossed him a piece of yellow fruit. Mark put the small end in his mouth. There was no way he could win the race now but he was determined not to finish last.

He yelled encouragement to his beast and kicked as hard as he could. The gray lunged down the track. It moved even with a group of riders, then slowly pushed past them.

In the distance Mark could see Dagon standing on the rail fence. The gray beast crossed the finish line just ahead of the final group of riders.

Mark spotted Sarbo. He spit out the pagoma and walked his mount over to him. "I guess you beat me. You want the necklace now?"

Sarbo threw his hands up. "I would be glad to take it except for the fact that the fruit dropped from my mouth and I was disqualified. So it is I who have lost the bet."

Mark shook his head. "We'll call it even, then."

The last rider had crossed the line and Dagon was announcing the winner. Sarbo looked disgusted. "Ha! Do you see that? The winner is Narqua. I beat him back here by a mile. If only I hadn't opened my mouth when I neared the finish."

The crowd cheered the announcement and congratulated the young man. Dagon clapped him on the back and presented him with a wreath of woven leaves.

Several animals filed by, heading back toward the village. Mark noticed one in particular, a large black.

"Sarbo. Who is the rider of that black?"

"I do not know. He is not from here. The Merkon brought him. Why do you ask?"

"During the race it felt as if someone pushed me off my mount. And when I was down, that rider tried to trample me."

Sarbo cocked his head. "This is your first race, Kakon. In the past I have seen riders become very reckless. One time a contestant was dragged to death. These things happen. You must not take it personally."

"Everything happened so fast, but I guess you have a

point. But what could have hit me hard enough to knock me off?"

Sarbo laughed. "The way you ride, I would say it was probably a feather."

"Very funny." Mark put his heels to his mount. "Maybe you would like to make a wager on the next game?"

"Be careful, Kakon. The next time you may not be so lucky."

chapter 33

The next game reminded Mark of a cross between football and King of the Mountain, except that the Tsook used the head of a pig-animal instead of a ball and it was every man for himself. The winner was the one who retrieved the head from a wooden bucket fifty yards from the starting line, ran back to a small circle in the center of the field and kept anyone else from taking it away.

Mark's back was still sore from his ride so he played only halfheartedly. Again he noticed that Megaan was not in the crowd of spectators.

The first man to get to the head dropped it and it was immediately scooped up by someone else. The players chased the second man until he stumbled and the head rolled out of his hands. Sarbo grabbed it and raced back to the circle. Another man tried to wrestle it away and pieces of pig head went everywhere.

Sarbo managed to hold on to the skull. Two men charged him and knocked him flying. He hit the ground and the rest piled on top.

When Dagon pulled the last man off, Sarbo was curled up, still holding what was left of the mangled head. Dagon declared him the winner.

Later Sarbo found Mark standing by one of the food tables. "It is a very good thing you did not bet against me this time, Kakon. As I predicted, I am the winner."

"If smelling like rotted brains makes you the winner, then you're right. You won."

Sarbo took a deep breath and grimaced. "I see what you mean. I suppose I must wash. Tell them not to start the next game until I come back."

Mark picked up a piece of bread. He munched on it thoughtfully. It was strange that none of the Merkon's men had participated in the game. He wondered why.

"There are more games later, Kakon." Barow ran up to him. "Are you going to enter the buffalo ride?"

"Sounds a little risky to me."

"I know you are only joking. You are not afraid of anything."

"Who told you that?" Mark swallowed a bite of bread. "I get afraid just like everybody else."

"Not like everyone else. When I am afraid I find a good place to hide."

"I've done that a few times. Speaking of hiding, where is your sister? I haven't seen her all day."

"She is not feeling well. The last time I saw her she was lying on her mat. And she must hurt bad because I think she was crying. It was probably something she ate last night."

"Really?" Mark shoved the rest of the bread into his mouth and started up the path.

"Where are you going, Kakon? The next event is about to start."

"Do me a favor and go tell them to wait for Sarbo."

"What about you?"

"I think I'll sit this one out. Hurry. Sarbo won't be too happy if they start without him."

Mark made his way to Dagon's cabin and knocked on the door. Megaan's grandmother opened it. "Hello, Kakon. Dagon is not here. I think you will find him at the buffalo pens selecting a bull for the games."

"I did not come to see Dagon. I heard Megaan is sick."

"Let him in, Grandmother," Megaan called.

Mark stepped inside. Megaan was sitting at the table shelling beans. He smiled. "You don't look sick."

Megaan's look was cross. "What do you want?"

"Me? Nothing, I just came to see how you were. Barow told me you were sick."

"You should not concern yourself." Megaan cracked open one of the hard orange pods. "After all, you will be leaving for the jungle soon. What is it to you if I am sick?"

"So that's what this is all about. You're still upset with me. Well, you're wrong. I'm not going to the jungle. At least not right now. Tomorrow the Merkon is taking me to Trisad to see a shaman friend of his."

Megaan put down her beans. "The Merkon? Why would he do this?"

"It was probably something you said—"

"What are you talking about?"

"The Merkon knows all about my past and my wanting to find the light. You and Leeta are the only ones who know about that."

"Th-Then it must have been her," Megaan sputtered. "I didn't tell anybody."

"Except me." Megaan's grandmother sat down at the end of the bench. "I am the one who talked to the Merkon about you. He stayed with us last night and questioned me about you. I did not think it would do any harm to tell him what I knew."

"Grandmother," Megaan scolded.

"Don't worry about it," Mark reassured her. "Actually, I think you did me a favor. The Merkon is going to help me. He knows a shaman who has seen the light and he is taking me to speak to him."

"I know of no shaman in Trisad," Megaan said. "Perhaps you heard him wrong."

"No. I'm sure it was Trisad." Mark picked up one of the pods. "After I find out where the light is, maybe I will come back and visit before I go to the jungle."

"If you wish." Megaan shrugged.

Mark stepped to the door. "If you're feeling better, Megaan, I hope you'll come to my ceremony tonight."

"Perhaps."

"Please?"

She looked up at him now and a smile came to her lips. "Perhaps . . ."

chapter 34

*Sarbo won the buffalo ride and the ax-*throwing contest. Now it was evening and the torches were lit again. The tables had been arranged in a circle around a large fire. More food had been prepared and the villagers had come out in droves to witness the initiation ceremony.

Mark wore his new white buckskins and was seated at the head table between Dagon and the Merkon. When the crowd settled down, Dagon stood and asked Mark to follow him to the middle of the circle.

Dagon held up his hands. "Tsook, behold the young warrior who has proven himself on the field of battle. He has been true to the people by offering his life for them."

A thunderous cheer went up from the tables. Mark scanned the spectators. Megaan wasn't there.

Dagon went on. "The Tsook are the original people. We are entrusted with Transall. Kakon has shown that he also wishes to be a guardian. If he is accepted, the Tsook pledge to be loyal to him, forsaking all they own to honor him. If he accepts the Tsook, he promises his loyalty to them, forsaking all he owns on their behalf."

It became strangely quiet. Mark waited anxiously. He had not been told what would happen next.

From a scabbard on his belt Dagon pulled a small hunting knife. "Kakon, do you still wish to be known as a warrior of the real people, the Tsook?"

Mark nodded.

Dagon took Mark's left hand and sliced the skin in the fleshy part of the palm. Mark winced as the warm blood dripped down his fingers.

"Who among you greets Kakon as Tsook and fellow warrior of Transall?"

There was a rumbling around the circle. Sarbo stepped up. "Let me be the first." Dagon made a similar cut on Sarbo's palm and the large man grabbed Mark's bloody hand and shook it vigorously. "I vow to protect you as Tsook to the best of my ability, Kakon." Sarbo moved away and Mark was surprised to see a long line of men waiting to do the same.

A lump rose in Mark's throat. The last man to make the vow was Dagon. The leader cut his own hand. "I am convinced it is no accident that you are here, Kakon. Surely you are destined for many great things. I am as glad for you today as if you were my own son."

Sarbo started the dancing. He moved around the fire to the rhythm of the drums. The others joined him until there was hardly any room to stand. Mark glanced around at the nearly empty tables. He saw Leeta taking Barow home but Megaan was still nowhere in sight. *Well—so she didn't come,* he thought. *Well.* He joined in with the dancers and tried to forget about her.

The dancing lasted for hours, until finally Dagon got everyone's attention and called for the last part of the ceremony.

"Kakon, if you will be seated, the people of the village will further show their acceptance and respect to you by presenting you with gifts." Dagon reached under his cape. "This crossbow is for you."

"But this is the one you just finished," Mark protested. "You've worked hard on it."

"And it is my gift to you. Kill many of our enemies with it."

Tybor stepped forward. "This is my gift, Kakon. See, I have finished it." He held out the metal breastplate and helmet. "Do you like it?"

Mark put the helmet on. "It fits, Tybor. You are a genius."

The Merkon sat up and fingered the breastplate. "This is good workmanship, blacksmith. How did you come to know how to make this?"

Tybor looked at Mark. "Kakon gave me instructions. He is very wise."

"I see that he is."

"Get out of the way, Tybor. You are not the only one with a gift." Sarbo pushed him aside. "Here is mine." He handed Mark his new sword.

Mark took it carefully. "I don't know what to say. This is a very special gift, Sarbo."

Sarbo winked at him. "The way you fight, I thought it only right to give you every advantage."

The Merkon clapped his hands. "I have a gift for you also, Kakon." One of his men led the Merkon's muscular silver-colored beast into the circle. "This animal was chosen from among the best stock in all Transall. It is yours."

Mark walked around the table and took the reins. "It is a wonderful gift. I thank you, Merkon." The animal snorted and danced sideways. Mark stroked its neck. "We will be good friends, you and I."

The rest of the villagers brought gifts and laid them at his feet. There was everything from food to blankets, and Mark thanked each individual.

Barow trotted up to him, out of breath. "I have a gift for you, Kakon. I did not make it but I think you will like it."

"Since it is from you, I am sure I will."

Barow handed him a folded rabbit skin tied with a vine. "Look inside, Kakon."

Mark had started to open it when Leeta walked up. "There you are, Barow. Your grandmother is very angry at you. Why did you sneak out of the house? You were supposed to be asleep hours ago."

Barow hung his head. "I just wanted to give Kakon a present like everyone else."

"Can't he stay just another minute?" Mark asked.

Leeta shook her head. "He and I will be in much trouble if I don't get him home right away."

Mark leaned down. "Tell you what. I'll wait until tomorrow, when you can watch me open it, okay?"

"All right," Barow said, pouting. He let Leeta lead him up the road. He yelled over his shoulder, "Do not forget, Kakon."

"I won't." Mark waved to him.

Sarbo staggered over. "The dancing has started again. Come, Kakon. Let us see if you can at least dance."

"I think you have had too much wild berry juice, Sarbo. You'd better leave the dancing to the younger men."

"Younger men," Sarbo growled. "I will have you know . . ." He fell backward into one of the tables and sat down on a bench. "I will have you know . . . that for once, perhaps you are right."

chapter 35

Mark was awake early, packing his things for the trip. He made a bedroll out of the blankets he had received and put some of the bread and dried food in a leather pouch.

His gifts were laid out on the table. He filled the water skin and admired the rest. One man had given him a basket of seed for planting his new field. It would be so easy to stay and let things go on the way they were.

He tried on the helmet and breastplate, put the sword into his belt and picked up the crossbow. He felt like a king. Everything he would ever need he now owned.

He carried his supplies outside and tied them on his new animal. The village was wide awake. Thin wisps of smoke rose from some of the houses and he could smell food cooking.

Sarbo's stocky brown beast trotted up. "I just got the news, Kakon. Dagon tells me you are already going on a quest."

"You could call it that. The Merkon is taking me to Trisad. There is an old shaman there I need to talk to."

Sarbo rubbed his chin. "Trisad? I did not know that broken-down place still existed. I have not been in that direction for many years. Perhaps I will ride along with you."

Mark looked at him suspiciously. "Why would you do that? Did Dagon order you to go?"

Sarbo pounded his chest with his large fist. "I am Tsook. I go where I please. Besides, an infant like yourself would not last long in the desert without a real warrior to protect him."

Mark sighed. "To tell you the truth, Sarbo, I'd be glad of the company. But not because I need protecting, only because the Merkon and his men seem so strange."

"Then it is settled. I will be back when I have collected my supplies." Sarbo whipped his beast and trotted down the road, passing the Merkon and six of his men.

Mark waited for them to ride up. "I'm almost ready, Merkon. Where are the rest of your men?"

The Merkon gave his reins to one of the riders and stepped down. "Since we are leaving by a different route, I have sent them on ahead to scout the area for enemies. We will meet up with them later."

He walked around Mark, inspecting his armor. "You could pass for one of my escorts. Perhaps, if you do not find what you are looking for in Trisad, you will consider joining me permanently?"

Mark avoided the question. "A friend is coming with us. I hope that is all right."

The Merkon stiffened. "It is unnecessary. My men will see to your every need. They will accompany you anywhere you wish to go. No harm will befall you."

"I appreciate that. But if it's not too much trouble, my friend wants to ride along with us. He has not been to Trisad in a long time."

"Mark." Leeta waved to him. "Barow is coming to watch you open his gift."

Mark had almost forgotten about the small rabbit skin. It was inside on the table.

Barow trotted up to him. "Megaan has a gift for you too."

Mark glanced up. Megaan was walking toward them, carrying something under her arm. When she got there she held it out. "I had some extra time so I made these."

Mark held up a pair of knee-length moccasins. "Thank you, Megaan. I haven't had shoes for a long time." He tried one on. "It fits. How did you know what size to make them?"

"She measured your footprint in the dirt," Barow answered.

Mark pulled the second moccasin on. It felt soft but odd. It had been almost three years since he had lost his hiking boot in the jungle. His feet had grown hard and callused.

He walked a few steps in them. "Now I really do have everything." He turned to Megaan. "Thank you. I missed you last night."

"I had to work on these moccasins."

"They are a wonderful gift. Thank you again." There was a moment when their eyes seemed almost to touch, a long moment. Then it was gone.

"Now open *my* present, Kakon." Barow pulled him to the cabin.

"Yes," Mark said. "Everyone come in and see the great gift my little friend Barow has given me."

Leeta and Megaan followed them inside. The Merkon stood in the doorway.

Mark sat down at the table and picked up the rabbit skin. "See all these things, Barow?"

The little boy nodded.

"I want you to take care of them while I'm away. And I need you to do me another big favor. Will you take the gray beast? It needs a good owner and now I don't have any use for it. Can you do that for me?"

Barow's eyes widened. "Do you mean it? I can have the gray for my own?"

"I mean it. But only if you take good care of it."

"I will, Kakon. You can count on me."

"Good. Now let's see what this can be." Mark cut the vine on the package and unfolded the skin.

Inside was a bluish piece of glass.

Mark was astonished. He'd had no idea these people knew how to make glass. He turned it over in his hand. There were letters printed on the bottom:

PRODUCT OF THE COCA-COLA COMPANY

3

chapter 36

He was on Earth.

It was incredible. It was impossible. He'd thought of it, of course—all the similarities: people who looked almost the same, plants almost the same, animals almost the same. But he'd decided that perhaps life on all livable planets had evolved more or less the same way—all from star stuff. He had been sure he was on a different planet.

But now there could be no doubt. He was still so stunned by the knowledge that he rode along among the Merkon's men hardly paying attention to where they were going.

The previous day he had delayed his departure for Trisad while he questioned Barow, Dagon and some of the older people. At first they weren't much help. To them, the world they lived in was called Transall, and they didn't care about the writing on the odd piece of glass.

Then Barow told him of other things with letters on them that the villagers had found over the years. Until Barow, no one in the village knew about reading, so the finders assumed that the strange marks were symbols left by earlier tribes.

Mark had insisted on seeing the artifacts. They brought him a small tube made of a tough transparent material, which bore the initials USAF, and a large chunk of steel that seemed to have no special origin until he scraped off the dirt and read the words GENERAL MOTORS. One woman had a perfect half of a white glass bowl with PYREX imprinted on the bottom. And an elderly man showed him a brass doorknob that he used for a handle on his walking stick with MADE IN JAPAN stamped on the bottom.

Now Mark was even more determined to see the shaman in Trisad. If Mark had come through some sort of time warp and been projected far into the future, he had to know if it was possible to go back.

Questions flooded his mind. What had happened to civilization and its technology? Where were all the cities and their billions of inhabitants? And what had caused the mutations in the plants, animals and people?

Whatever had happened, Mark mused, it must have been catastrophic. The Tsook people had regressed to the Dark Ages, the arrow people even further, and the Rawhaz were barely above wild animals.

Mark let his mount fall back to the end of the procession. The Merkon's men watched him but didn't say anything. Sarbo circled back and rode up beside him.

"What is troubling you, infant? You have been acting strange all day."

"It's a long story. I'm not sure you would believe me if I told you." Mark looked at the big man. There was genuine concern on his wide yellow face.

"Sarbo, have you ever heard of a fantastic light with more power than a bolt of lightning? Power to transport people across time?"

Sarbo stroked his short black beard thoughtfully. "Is this what your quest is about? Are you trying to find this light?"

Mark lowered his voice and chose his words carefully. "I came to Transall with the aid of that light. I belong to a time hundreds, no probably thousands, of years in the past."

Sarbo's eyes widened and Mark hurriedly continued. "I know it's hard to believe. I had a rough time with it myself. But now I have proof. The glass present Barow gave me with the writing on it belongs to my time. So do those other old things they brought to my cabin yesterday."

"It is true that you are different. That much I know." Sarbo paused and glanced up to the head of the column of men. "Dagon noticed it right away. There has been only one other . . ." He stopped.

"One other?" Mark repeated. "You mean you've seen someone else who looks like me?"

"Yes, I—"

An arrow slammed into the shoulder of Sarbo's beast. The animal screamed and reared, pawing the air with its front legs. More arrows followed, sticking in the ground all around them.

"Run for the woods, Kakon!" Sarbo turned his animal and bolted to the right. A battery of arrows flew at them from the trees.

"We have to go back," Sarbo yelled. "Stay with me, Kakon."

Mark jerked his beast around and thundered after Sarbo at full speed.

Without warning Sarbo darted off the path. Mark sped after him through the deep red grass and into the forest.

In the cover of the trees Sarbo slid to the ground and skillfully twisted and pulled the arrow from the beast's flesh. Blood squirted out and streamed down the animal's leg. Sarbo poured a little water in the dirt and made a mud poultice.

Mark grabbed his sword and stood guard near the edge of the woods.

They could hear shouts, but no one came after them. Sarbo put his fingers to his lips, motioning for Mark to remain quiet. Even after silence had settled they continued to wait in the trees.

After almost an hour Sarbo finally spoke. "It was an ambush. Our attackers were waiting for us, Kakon."

"How can you be sure?" Mark whispered. "No one could have known the Merkon was going to Trisad. He only decided himself two days ago."

"I am sure. Come, let us see if there are any survivors."

Sarbo checked his beast's wound. The poultice had stopped the bleeding. He climbed on its back and cautiously entered the clearing. Mark trotted up beside him, listening intently for anything out of the ordinary. When they reached the spot where they had been attacked they discovered three of the Merkon's men sprawled on the ground, dead.

"The Merkon must have gotten away!" Mark exclaimed. "At least, if they killed him it didn't happen here." He turned and noticed Sarbo examining one of the bodies. "What is it? Did you find something?"

"Perhaps." Sarbo broke the shaft off the arrow sticking out

of the man's neck and brought it to Mark. "Do you recognize this?"

"Rawhaz." Mark frowned. "I didn't know they planned their attacks. An organized ambush doesn't seem to be their style."

"It is not their way. They come upon their enemy and fight to the death. It was not the Rawhaz who ambushed us today. Look carefully at the design. It is hastily painted on. The Rawhaz take pride in creating their weapons. And they are scavengers. They would never leave these swords and crossbows lying here in the dirt. No, whoever finds these bodies is supposed to be fooled into believing this was the work of the Rawhaz. But it was not."

chapter 37

They had picked up the trail of the Merkon's beast. It appeared that the Merkon had been captured by an army of several dozen men. They followed the tracks for three or four miles before losing them in a dense wood.

At dark Sarbo found a secluded spot and suggested they camp for the night. He reapplied the mud poultice to his beast's wound and settled down to a cold camp, deciding it would be better not to build a fire until they knew more about the danger of their situation.

Mark sank his teeth into a hard piece of bread, chewed twice and swallowed. "Who do you think went to all the trouble to make the attack look as if it came from the Rawhaz? And why would they do it? Does the Merkon have enemies?"

Sarbo lay back in the grass. "The Merkon is . . . an unusual man. He has been able to unite all the Tsook as one people. No one else has ever done this. But there are some who resent him."

"Some of the Tsook?"

"Half Tsook. In the long ago time when there were not so many real people, one tribe of Tsook captured an entire race of desert dwellers called the Samatin. They intermarried with them and their children became half-breeds, no longer true Tsook."

"What does this have to do with the Merkon?"

"The Merkon has declared that the Samatin are not to be considered part of us. Their lands are not under Tsook protection and may be plundered for the good of the real people."

"Sounds like bigotry is still alive and well on this planet," Mark muttered.

"I do not understand."

Mark shook his head. "Did it ever occur to you that the Samatin are people like you? Why hate them just because they are another race? And what about me? I'm not true Tsook."

"You have earned the right to be Tsook."

"This is an impossible conversation." Mark tore off another piece of bread and chewed on it thoughtfully. Sarbo was set in his ways and there was no talking him out of them. Mark decided to change the subject. "How far is Trisad from here?"

"Two, maybe three days. It is in the middle of the Death Sand. Long ago one of the tribes created a city there made completely of mud bricks. It was a trading center for caravans on the way to the river. But it is almost gone now and only a few people live there. Mostly those who are in hiding or wish to be left alone."

Mark finished his bread. "What do you think will happen to the Merkon?"

"If it was the Rawhaz who attacked us he is dead by now. But if, as I suspect, it was the Samatin, they are holding him for a ransom."

"Should we go on looking for him?"

"We will keep our eyes open for tracks. But I think it is no use to go after them. By now they have already determined his fate. Tomorrow we will go to Trisad."

Mark leaned back. "If something happens to the Merkon, who will take his place as Overlord of the Tsook?"

"That I do not know. The Merkon governs from a large city across the river called Listra. I am sure there are many of his officers there who could take over. I have heard he has a son. But they say he has deliberately never appointed anyone as second in command."

"Perhaps when they are paid, the Samatin will release the Merkon and no one will have to worry about it," Mark said. He raised himself on his elbows. "Just before the attack you were telling me that you have seen someone who looks like me. Someone both you and Dagon know. Who is it?"

Sarbo cleared his throat. "Never before had we seen round eyes like yours, or light skin, or feet without a protective covering on the bottom. Then many years ago such a man came to our village. Like you, he earned the right to become Tsook. He was smart and very strong, and soon he became a powerful warrior."

"Who was this man?"

"The Merkon."

chapter 38

The crystals in the red sand reflected the sun's sweltering rays, and beads of sweat trickled down Mark's forehead. He wanted to take a drink from his almost-empty leather pouch but Sarbo had already warned him that they should use their small supply of water sparingly.

Sarbo had explained that many who had wandered through the Death Sand had never returned to their homes and families. Some went out, lost their way and became crazy with thirst. Others simply vanished.

The arid landscape was a stark change from the mountains and jungle. Even the treeless plains of the Rawhaz were inviting compared to this. There was no vegetation to be seen in any direction, nothing but endless scarlet sand.

Sarbo's beast was still recovering from its shoulder wound and moved at a stiff gait. Mark's animal plodded alongside, not wanting to move any faster either because of the suffocating heat.

The night before, they had camped near a small water hole. It was the only one Sarbo knew of on the way to

Trisad. Mark used the time to question him about the Merkon. Where was his tribe? Had he ever said whether there were more like him?

Sarbo didn't have any answers. He and Dagon had been young men when they had first met the Merkon and noticed how different he was. It had been more than twenty-five years ago. As for the Merkon's background, the Overlord told them he came from a tribe of metal workers from across the great waters.

Mark assumed that was the ocean. He asked Sarbo if he had ever seen it. Sarbo laughed and said he did not believe such a thing existed. So Mark drew him a crude map of the world in the sand. In North America he carefully depicted all the rivers and mountains he could remember and explained where the land stopped and the ocean began. He told Sarbo about the great ships that sailed from one continent to the next.

Sarbo was hard to convince until Mark drew the Rockies and the Rio Grande. The big man seemed to recognize them and after that he grew oddly quiet and sullen.

Today he was still not very talkative. Mark chalked it up to the heat. They traveled mile after mile in silence.

Mark had long since taken off his armor and tied it around his beast's neck. It reflected the sun's rays and clanked lightly as they walked. He was considering letting it drop in the sand when Sarbo pulled his animal to a sharp stop.

"I have been thinking about what you told me, Kakon. Your story about the light must be true. No one in Transall possesses the kind of knowledge you have. Therefore, you are surely not from our world. I will do what I can to help you return to yours."

"Thank you, Sarbo. I appreciate your vote of confidence. You've already been a big help. I know I couldn't have come this far without you."

Sarbo pointed ahead. "Trisad is just over that far rise. If the shaman you are looking for is not there, we will not stop until we find him."

Mark rubbed his sweaty chin on his shirt sleeve. As he did, he happened to glance back and saw a small red cloud of dust moving up fast.

"Looks like we're about to have company."

Sarbo turned. The expression on his face changed. "Samatin. No one else could move that quickly in the Death Sand. Hurry, Kakon. We must make it to Trisad before they catch us."

They whipped their beasts and moved out across the sand. The Samatin were gaining on them. The pursuers were riding short, fast-moving animals, and the deep sand didn't seem to slow them much. Mark could see the outline of the front rider. A white cloth was wrapped around his head turban-style and his sheetlike clothing flapped like giant wings as he rode.

The rise Sarbo had pointed to earlier seemed to be moving away from them. Mark urged his beast to go faster.

Sarbo's injured mount stumbled and its leg folded underneath it. The warrior lost his seat and rolled across the sand. He scrambled to his feet. "Go on, Kakon. Hurry. You can make it. I will hold them off as long as I can."

Mark ground to a stop and jerked his beast around.

"Don't be foolish, Sarbo. Get on behind me. Either we both make it or neither of us does."

Sarbo hesitated, then quickly swung on behind Mark. The silver animal turned and ran, but it was held back by the sand and the added weight.

The Samatin were closing in. There were more than twenty of them, whooping and hollering in choppy cries.

Mark finally topped the rise. Below them he saw the ruins of an old adobe city. The walls were crumbling and whole sections were missing. He drove the beast down a steep sand dune and charged through the high broken wall that had once surrounded the city.

"We can make our stand here," Mark said as he pulled the beast to a stop. He reached for his sword and crossbow, then jumped down and ran to the wall.

The Samatin had spread out in a line across the top of the dune. They raised their curved swords and yelled what sounded like jeers and threats. A few of them shot arrows in the direction of the wall but the arrows fell short by several yards.

"What are they doing?" Mark stared up at them. "Taunting us?"

Sarbo watched the Samatin through a large hole in the wall. "No. If what I have heard is correct, I believe they are afraid."

"Afraid? Of what? They have us outnumbered ten to one."

"They are not afraid of you and me. They are afraid of this place. In the before times, Trisad was known as an important religious center. A variety of worshipers converged here for sacred rites, and from them the Samatin's own beliefs sprang up. They consider this place untouchable. Holy ground."

"Are you saying that they're superstitious? As long as we are here, they won't come in after us?"

"Yes. But do not forget, they are the sworn enemy of the Tsook. We will not be allowed to leave alive. They will be waiting for us."

"We'll worry about that when the time comes." Mark turned his back on the shrill yells of the Samatin. "Let's go find the shaman."

chapter 39

Trisad's dusty main street was desolate.
The only sign of life was a filthy beggar with a gray beard
that almost touched the ground. He sat in rags near one of
the fallen-down houses, and when they walked by he
pleaded for scraps of food.

Mark peered into the dark opening of one of the buildings. Several large burbbas, rat creatures, scurried across the
floor. Up the street a door slammed. A small breeze kicked
up a red whirlwind that blew itself out against one of the
ancient weather-beaten walls.

A thin woman darted across the road in front of them,
balancing a basket on her head. Mark couldn't help noticing
a wide scar on her face that ran from her left eyebrow down
to her chin.

"Friendly place," Mark said.

"I told you, Kakon, Trisad is now a refuge for outlaws and
others who want to remain hidden. People here keep to
themselves, and they do not like outsiders. Come, I know a

man who will give us food and drink. When the time is right, I will ask him about the shaman."

Sarbo turned a corner and stepped into a yard littered with bones and broken pottery. A furry animal on a short chain, a cross between a dog and an alligator, snarled at Mark's beast. "Wait here, Kakon. I will see if we are welcome."

Sarbo strode into the shadows. Mark watched him walk down a set of dirt steps and heard him knock vigorously on a door.

"Hello to the Short Man," he shouted. "Out here in the hot sun you have Sarbo the warrior."

There was no answer. Mark led his beast to the edge of the steps to get a better look. Sarbo shrugged and then knocked again. "Short Man, I come with a friend. We require food and shelter for the night. Dare you turn us away?"

The door creaked open less than an inch. A deep voice boomed out, "Sarbo? Is it really you?"

"Open the door, you old fool, before I break it down around your ears."

"It must be you. Only Sarbo would be brash enough to threaten Trisad's greatest fighting man." The door swung open and a portly man with a shaved head and a barrel chest stepped out. He threw his arms around Sarbo, pounded on his back and then stepped away, grinning. "I heard you were killed in a Rawhaz raid, you son of a garka snake."

"Lies. All lies," Sarbo said, laughing. "Like the one about you being a great fighting man."

"Who is your companion?" Short Man nodded toward

Mark. "I have not seen his kind before. Strange-looking sort."

"Never mind about his looks. He is a true friend, brave of heart, and not too bad in a fight either. We need a place to stay tonight. Will you take us?"

Short Man yelled into the house, "Yonk, get out here. Take their mount and see that it is well taken care of."

A scrawny boy nine or ten years old with smudges of dirt on his face awkwardly rushed up the steps. He took the reins from Mark and led the beast away.

"Come inside, my old friend. There is plenty of rodent soup on the fire." Short Man led the way down more steps into a musty cellar.

There were no windows in the underground room. Light came from a pot of burning oil hanging in the corner and from a small, round adobe fireplace. Rugs were strewn about on the floor to serve as furniture. Sarbo sat down on one and Mark did the same.

Short Man lifted the lid off a tall pot and pulled out a gourd dipper full of lukewarm water. He handed it to Sarbo, waited until he had drunk his fill, then offered some to Mark.

There was something about this loud man Mark didn't like. He couldn't quite put his finger on it but he definitely felt uneasy about him.

The boy called Yonk timidly slunk back into the room and sat down in a dark corner.

Short Man glared at him. "Do not sit, ignorant dung. Get our guests some food. Can't you see they have come a long way and are extremely hungry?"

The boy went to the pot hanging over the fire. He

scooped some stew into two wooden bowls and handed one to Sarbo. He turned to hand the other one to Mark. When he did, some of it slopped over the edge and landed on Mark's foot.

"Fool!" Short Man bellowed. He raised his hand to strike the boy but Mark jumped between them.

"There is no harm done," Mark said quietly, his hand on the hilt of his sword. "It was an accident. Do not tire yourself by beating this slave on my account."

Yonk's eyes were wide with fear. Silence filled the room. Finally Short Man stepped back. "You are right, Sarbo. Your strange-looking friend is very brave. Either that or very foolish."

"He is young." Sarbo dismissed the incident with a wave of his hand. "Let us talk of other things."

"Yes." Short Man sat down. "Let us discuss why you have come to this forsaken desert. Surely it is not just to see an old friend?"

"Ha!" Sarbo gulped a swallow of the hot stew. "If you think that, then the heat has finally addled your brains. No, we are looking for someone. We have come to see a shaman who has been residing in Trisad."

"Shaman?" Short Man slapped his knee. "That is a very funny joke."

Mark started to speak but Sarbo held his hand up in warning and continued. "We were told that there was a shaman here who had knowledge of strange powers. One who had seen some extraordinary things and could give us some information we are seeking."

"I don't know who told you this, my friend." Short Man was still chuckling. "But they have made fools of you. You came all this way for nothing. There is no shaman here now, and there never has been."

"Perhaps he is not a shaman," Mark said. "It is possible that we heard wrong. Perhaps there is someone here who used to be a medicine man. Someone who knows about the before time?"

"*Psshh.* Who cares about that?" Short Man leaned forward. "Now tell me why you are really here, Sarbo. Are you on the run? Scouting ahead for a raid? If the booty is good I might be persuaded to go along."

Sarbo hesitated briefly. "I knew I would not be able to fool you, Short Man." He set his bowl on the dirt floor. "The fact is, we were doing some scouting and ran into the Samatin. I lost my beast and we came here to see if I could pick up another."

Short Man rubbed his thick hands together. "A trade? What do you have?"

"We will talk about it in the morning, my friend. Now I am very tired. When we have rested we will start the bargaining."

"Of course, what was I thinking? Yonk, show our guests to the stables. They will get a good night's sleep and then"— Short Man opened the door—"tomorrow we will bargain."

chapter **40**

"Sir, wake up."

Mark felt someone gently shaking his shoulder. His eyes flew open. Yonk was kneeling next to him. The boy put his fingers to his lips and motioned for Mark to follow him outside.

It was still dark and Mark had a hard time keeping up with the boy. Yonk led him through a narrow alley and into an abandoned storehouse.

Inside, Yonk lit a small torch. "You are in much danger, sir. I could easily lose my life for telling you this."

"Then why are you telling me?"

"Because you stood up to him. No one has ever done that. You must be very brave."

"Why am I in danger?"

"Everyone in Trisad knew you were coming. There has been a reward offered for your capture. Short Man hopes to keep you here long enough to collect it."

Mark scratched his head. "A reward? Why would anybody put out a reward for me?"

"That I do not know. But if you stay here you will regret it. Take your friend and go back to your village at once." Yonk blew out the torch and started for the door.

Mark grabbed his arm. "Wait! Tell me, is it true that there is no shaman living in Trisad?"

"Short Man did not lie. There is no one like that here. But there is someone who speaks about the before time. He is very old and they say he has lost his mind. I doubt you could understand anything he says."

"Get him. I have to talk to this person. It is very important to me."

Yonk fidgeted with the torch. "This will not be easy. I have already saved your life. Why should I do this also?"

"I can't explain. But if you do it I will owe you a great deal."

"Really? How much in trade goods?"

"Go get the old man, you little wretch," Sarbo's deep voice demanded from the open door. "And hurry up about it or I will crush your head as if it was an overripe melon."

Yonk squeezed past him and ran down the alley.

"Did you hear everything?" Mark asked.

"Almost." Sarbo stepped inside. "It seems that you have become a wanted man."

"They have me confused with someone else."

"Of course. I forgot for a moment how much like everyone else you look. I am sure it is just a big mistake."

"I guess you have a point there. But what else could it be? Up until a few days ago no one here even knew I existed."

"Someone did. The Merkon heard about you. And when he found out he made a special trip across many miles just to meet you."

Mark was quiet, thinking. The Merkon had told him there was a shaman here. Why would he lie?

"There is something not right about this, Kakon. I said I will help you in your quest and I will, but we are at a disadvantage. First we must find out who our enemies are and know all that is going on."

There was a noise at the door. Yonk led in the old beggar they had seen asking for food on the street the day before. "This is the man, masters. He is called Pet. Talk to him if you can."

Mark helped the feeble old man find a place to sit. "We need light, Yonk. I want to see who I'm talking to."

Yonk hit two small rocks together and relit the oiled rag on the end of his torch.

Mark knelt beside the man and looked into his face. It was wrinkled and caked with dirt and his matted hair hung down over his eyes. "I need to ask you some questions, Pet. Do you understand me?"

There was no response. Mark continued. "They say you know about the before time. Can you tell me about it?"

"I know much about the before time," Pet squeaked in a dry, raspy voice. "But you do not really care. You are one of the carriers of the long death. You have the look."

"The look?" Mark asked quietly. "What can you tell me about my looks?"

Pet stared straight ahead. "I am the last of the keepers. When I die it will all be lost."

"What will be lost, Pet? What do you keep?"

"The knowledge. The ancients entrusted it to my family. We have always been keepers."

"Do you know about a light, Pet? A great light that can take you to a different time?"

The man covered his head with his arms and rocked back and forth. "So much waste and destruction. Many suffered through the long death. So many died that the bodies were piled up and there was no one left to sing the songs. When the blood sick came to this land it spread like a fire. No one was safe." He stopped rocking. "It could still be out there. Be careful."

Yonk shook his head. "I told you he was crazy. You will find out nothing from him. I had better take him back now."

"Wait." Mark put his hand on the old man's shoulder. "This is important, Pet. What do you know about a powerful light that appears in the jungle?"

"The people did not know how to grow food or defend themselves. Only handfuls survived and they were changed. Everything was changed in the blood sick."

"He is rambling, Kakon." Sarbo glanced out the door. "It will be morning soon. We must go."

Frustrated, Mark looked back at Pet. "I know you are trying to tell me what happened in Transall to make everything different from my time. But I don't understand all that. All I want to know about is the light. Can you tell me anything about the light?"

The old man stared at the torch without blinking.

"It is no use, Kakon." Sarbo helped the old man to his feet. "Take him back to his house, Yonk. And"—he grabbed the boy's arm—"do not go back to the Short Man tonight. It could prove to be dangerous."

Sarbo waited until they had gone and turned to Mark. "Come with me. Before this night is over we will have some answers."

chapter 41

Sarbo stepped back, took a deep breath and slammed his body into the door. It splintered, fell off its leather hinges and crashed, barely missing the sleeping man inside.

"Wha—What's going on?" Short Man frantically reached for his sword.

Mark kicked it across the room. Sarbo stepped on Short Man's chest, pushing him down as he held the blade of his sword against the man's neck.

"Sarbo," Short Man gulped. "My good friend. What is the meaning of this?"

"That is what we are here to find out, Short Man." Sarbo stepped down harder. "Light the oil pot, Kakon. The fire doesn't let me see into this deceiver's eyes."

"Deceiver? I would never deceive you, Sarbo. Someone has given you false information."

"There is a reward offered for the capture of my friend. Who is behind it?"

"I do not know what you are talking about. I—"

Sarbo pressed the blade into Short Man's flesh until he drew blood. "I have no time to waste. It will be daylight soon. If you value your life, tell me before I cut your head off and feed it to that corwunk on the chain outside."

Short Man closed his eyes. "All right. Someone came here. He said your odd-looking friend was worth a lot to someone very important."

"Who wants him? And why?"

"He did not give a name. All I know is that he rode a fine beast and wore metal armor like the kind tied to your friend's gear."

Mark gave a low whistle. "The Merkon."

"Or one of his men." Sarbo looked down at the white-faced man on the floor. "When did he say he would be back?"

"He did not say. Only that if we wanted the reward we had to hold him here until they came for him. I had no idea he was your companion, Sarbo. I just thought I could pick up some easy booty."

Sarbo stepped back. "I will not kill you, Short Man. My friend and I are leaving now. If you know what is good for you, you will stay out of our way. And if the man in armor returns it would be better for you if you do not tell him we were here."

"Of course." Short Man sat up and rubbed his throat. "I could never betray you, Sarbo. You know that."

"If the reward was large enough, you would betray anyone." Sarbo sheathed his sword. "But see to it that you do not or I will return. And next time, I promise that you will not be left attached to your head."

There was a sound in the courtyard. Mark blew the light out and moved silently up the steps.

Standing in front of him was his silver beast, along with a fat black one and a short, hairy animal like the kind the Samatin had been riding.

"See how I think ahead, master?" Yonk said to Mark, pulling the animals closer. "You could use someone like me on your journey."

"For what?" Sarbo climbed the steps. "You would only slow us down."

Yonk appealed to Mark. "Master, you know that if I stay here Short Man will kill me the minute you are out of sight. Haven't I stood by you from the start?"

Mark rubbed his chin thoughtfully.

"I can cook," Yonk went on. "And I am good with animals. I will see to your every need. You will not have to lift a finger. It would be a terrible mistake not to take me with you."

Sarbo took the reins of the black beast and jumped on its back. He looked at Mark. "Come, Kakon. Perhaps the Samatin are sleeping."

Mark climbed on his animal and followed Sarbo to the edge of the courtyard. He stopped and looked over his shoulder at Yonk. "If you are coming you'd better hurry. Nobody's going to wait for you."

"Oh, thank you, master." Yonk hopped on the small donkeylike animal and trotted after them. "I promise you will not regret this."

chapter 42

"*You are very crafty, masters.*" Yonk's animal jogged through the deep red sand, easily keeping pace with the larger beasts. "You have outsmarted the Samatin. Of course, I knew you would. Otherwise I would not have chosen to come with you."

Sarbo gave Mark a sullen glance. "Does that runt ever shut up?"

"I am sorry if I have offended you, master. I was just saying that it has been almost two days and you have managed to successfully elude the Samatin. It is not everyone who could have escaped their watchful eyes so easily."

"That is what worries me." Sarbo shifted his weight and glanced nervously around. "It seemed *too* easy."

"Why would they let us go?" Mark asked. "They wanted us pretty badly the other day."

"Who knows? Perhaps the runt is right. I am probably worrying for no reason. It will be dark soon. We will camp just over that next dune."

They plodded along in silence. Mark hoped he had made

the right decision. He had been the one to choose their destination—Listra. He felt sure the Merkon had the answers he was looking for—if the man was still alive. If not, there might be someone close to him who knew why he had taken such an interest in Mark. The only way to find out for certain was to go to his stronghold across the river in Listra and ask questions.

Sarbo had refused to consider going back to the village without Mark. And Yonk didn't seem to care which way they went, as long as it was away from Short Man.

"Look, masters! Trees!" Yonk pointed down the sand dune to a stand of short red trees. "We must be getting close to the end of the Death Sand. I had almost forgotten what they looked like. Aren't they beautiful? Are we going to camp there? It would be wonderful to have shade."

"If it will help to get you to close your flapping mouth, I would be willing to camp in a patch of thornspears," Sarbo said. He kicked his beast and moved out in front of them.

"I get the feeling he does not like me much," Yonk said in a low voice. "Have I done something to offend him? Have I not done everything in my power to please him?"

Mark urged his mount down the dune. "I think Sarbo is happy enough with your work. But from now on you might try doing it with a little less talk."

Sarbo had stopped. The trees were still ahead. Mark rode up to him, leaving Yonk behind. "Is something wrong?"

"It is too still." Sarbo studied the line of trees. "I don't like it, Kakon. We must turn back."

As he tugged on the rein, an arrow whizzed and struck Sarbo in the side. The big man slumped forward, hanging on to his beast's mane.

"Go!" Sarbo shouted hoarsely.

Mark reached for the reins of Sarbo's mount and tried to make a run for it, but a swarm of Samatin charged out of the trees and surrounded them before he had moved more than a few feet.

The leader, a filthy man wearing a stained white turban, gave them a grin that exposed his rotted front teeth. His look dared Mark to make a move against them.

Mark dropped the reins and slowly put his hands in the air. The Samatin began whooping. For several minutes they pranced around their captives, yelling and occasionally poking at Mark and Sarbo with their spears. Finally they took their captives' weapons and tied Mark's hands behind his back with a thin leather strap.

The language they spoke was even choppier than the arrow people's. Mark couldn't understand a word. They led the two beasts behind their hairy animals, obviously very pleased with themselves, chattering and waving their arms.

Mark chanced a quick glance up at the sand dune. Yonk was nowhere in sight.

The Samatin hadn't bothered to tie Sarbo. He was losing a lot of blood and could barely hang on to his beast.

Mark felt helpless. "Hold on, Sarbo," he whispered. "I'll get us out of this—somehow."

There was no answer.

Sweat trickled down Mark's forehead and stung his eyes. This was his fault. He should have insisted that Sarbo return to his village, and he should have gone back to the dark jungle. It had been a mistake to drag his friend into this mess.

A few miles later the Samatin dropped into a sandy canyon that got deeper and deeper. They followed it for almost an hour before they stopped in front of what appeared to be a solid wall of red rock and sand.

One by one they rode to the far side and disappeared around the edge. The man leading Mark's beast got off his animal and clicked a command. The little animal followed the others while he carefully led Mark and the bigger animal around the edge of the narrow opening.

Mark was amazed. The shimmering sand gave the illusion that there was no way through the wall. But once they rounded the opening there was a long, dark tunnel just wide enough for a beast to pass. He had to duck to avoid being scraped off by low-hanging rocks.

The darkness didn't slow the man leading Mark's mount. He seemed to know the way very well.

Just when Mark thought the tunnel would never end, a light appeared and the little man led him out into a valley.

Mark's eyes widened. The ground was black and the vegetation green. Green, the way he remembered it was supposed to be.

As they walked, a powdery dirt swirled up around the man's ankles. Mark looked down and saw that they were walking through old volcanic ash. The Samatin had founded their hidden paradise on the remains of an inactive volcano. The rim of the blackened cone loomed in front of them.

Women and children came out of their mud huts to stare at the prisoners. Dog creatures with long thin tails that dragged on the ground barked and nipped at the heels of the mounts.

The leader pointed at Sarbo and shouted. Two of the Samatin roughly pulled him, unconscious, off his beast and carried him into one of the huts. Then the leader gave another order and pointed at Mark.

A heavy blow hit Mark in the ribs and he fell, landing on his shoulder in the dirt.

The Samatin roared with laughter.

Mark struggled to his knees, his hands still tied. Someone kicked him solidly in the back and he fell on his face. He scrambled to his feet and warily watched the crowd to see who his next attacker would be.

It was the little man who had led his beast. He jumped at Mark, intending to jab him with his spear. Mark sidestepped, whirled and landed a kick to the short man's stomach.

The crowd stopped laughing. One of their own had been bested by a prisoner. They pressed in closer to see what would happen next.

The little man turned, his narrow black eyes flashing. He braced himself, raised the spear and charged again.

Mark was ready. He dropped to the ground and scissored his legs to trip the man. The small fellow was propelled forward into the crowd. The spear flew out of his hand and landed in the dirt near the leader.

The leader was not amused. He clapped his hands sharply and his men rushed to grab Mark. They took him to a small cage made of tree limbs and pushed him inside. There was a rope attached to the top; they threw it around a high tree branch and raised the cage off the ground.

The prison was not designed for someone as tall as Mark. When he sat flat on the floor, his head touched the top. The cage was so small there was hardly room for him to move. He studied the way it was built. The sturdy sticks were held in place by leather strips like the one that was cutting into his wrists.

He was carrying his old pocketknife in a pouch around his waist, but it was impossible to get to it.

The Samatin people had crowded around below the cage and were throwing rocks and spitting and jeering at him. Whatever he did, if anything, would have to wait until nightfall.

chapter **43**

*The night was warm and bright. The moon-*light shone through the haze better here than anywhere else Mark had been in Transall.

The Samatin had finally given up taunting him and gone into their huts to sleep. Wedged in his prison, Mark sat thinking, trying to take his mind off how uncomfortable he was.

Back in his world the sulfur from volcanoes had been used to make many things, particularly explosive powder. He racked his brain, trying to remember the formula.

His science teacher had talked about it. Mark had stored the information because he thought he and his friends might find it useful one day for homemade fireworks.

The Chinese or somebody had figured out that if you added the sulfur from pure deposits of brimstone to charcoal and potassium nitrate you could produce a potentially lethal explosion.

Mark smiled grimly. It was funny what you could remember in these bizarre situations. He continued to think. The charcoal was easy. It was right there in the residue of old fires the Samatin had let burn down. He suspected the long tunnel they came through had all the potassium nitrate he would need. But what was the formula?

There was a disturbance on the other side of the camp. In the moonlight he could see a Samatin guard on a mount, dragging someone behind him.

It was Yonk. The man picked up the boy and stuffed him into another cage. Then he raised it off the ground near Mark's.

"I tried to save you, master. Honestly, I did. I would have done it too, if it had not been for the tunnel guard. He is a coward and a thief. He came at me from behind and took my donkey and my pack. When I get out of here I will rip him apart. I will—"

"Yonk?"

"Yes, master?"

"Thank you for coming after us. It's good to see you. But if you don't mind, I'm trying to think right now."

"Are you about to come up with a grand plan to escape from these barbaric people along with Master Sarbo? Where is Master Sarbo? If you do have a plan I can be of great help to you. In fact, I once—"

"Yonk?"

"Yes, master?"

"Shut up."

"Yes, master."

Mark pulled his knees up under his chin. He inched onto his back and pushed upward with his feet. The round wooden bars didn't budge.

Next he tried bracing his back against one side of the cage

and his feet against the other. He pushed again with all his might but nothing happened.

"This is hopeless," he muttered. He looked up at the sky. The faint outline of a star shone through the haze. He hadn't seen a star since the night he had discovered the blue light more than three years ago, and for the first time in months he felt a twinge of homesickness.

"Yonk?"

"You asked me not to talk, master."

"Forget about that. Are your hands tied in the front or back?"

"They are tied in the front, master. That is how that Samatin coward was able to drag me along behind his mount. And, you know, I think he enjoyed it too. I heard him laughing."

"Listen to me. I'm going to tell you how the latch on your cage works. Put your hands through the bars and feel for a round wooden wheel."

"I have it, master."

"Turn the wheel to your left."

"I am trying. It will not turn. Something is holding it."

"Feel for a wooden peg in the face of the wheel. Pull it straight out."

"It still will not move, master."

"Rock the wheel back and forth. And pull harder, Yonk. Sarbo and I are counting on you."

Mark heard the cage gate snap open. "Good work, Yonk. Now jump down and lower my cage."

"Master, I am not very good with heights. What if I break my leg or worse, what if I fall on my—"

"Jump!"

"Yes, master."

Mark heard him hit the ground with a thud. "Are you all right?"

"Yes. Although I am not sure that you really care how I am, considering that I told you I did not like heights and—"

"Find the rope that holds my cage. When you do, let it out slowly."

"I found it, master," Yonk whispered. "But it is difficult to undo it with my hands tied together."

Mark's cage lurched downward. He closed his eyes and prepared for the crash.

It didn't come. The cage jerked to a stop. Mark opened his eyes to find himself suspended a few inches above the ground.

"Good work, Yonk. Now open my cage. Yonk?"

"I am up here, master."

Mark looked up. High in the tree, dangling from the end of the rope, was Yonk. He was holding on with both hands.

"Get down here, Yonk. I need you."

"But, master, it is a very long way to fall. Even farther than the last time."

"Yonk, if you don't get down here and unlock my cage someone will find us like this. And I hear the Samatin enjoy cooked Tsook. They say the younger the victim the more tender the meat."

There was another thud. This time it was accompanied by a soft groan.

"Do not worry, master. I am fine." Yonk's face appeared in front of Mark's cage. The boy turned the wheel and pulled out the peg, and the door sprang open.

"Reach in my pouch, Yonk, and find my small knife. Cut me loose and I will do the same for you."

Yonk found the knife and sawed at the strap until Mark was able to break it. "See, master. Did I not tell you that you would find me very useful?"

"You told me. Now quit talking and get your hands over here."

chapter 44

"But, master, does it not make more sense to steal back our animals and escape while we still have a chance? You raised our cages back into the tree. They will not discover we are gone for quite some time."

"Hand me that bowl of dirt, Yonk."

"That is exactly what I was saying, master. Here you are hiding behind bushes, sifting through dirt and grinding charred sticks to powder when we could be halfway to Listra by now. It was a very risky thing for you to send me back to the tunnel. I was very lucky the guard was away. And why did you have me do it? To escape? No. To collect dirt. I am sure there will be plenty of dirt in Listra, master. I will help you get all you want. Why do we not go?"

"I will not leave Sarbo. This may be the only way for the Samatin to know I mean business. Hand me that other bowl and spread that rag out beside it."

Yonk did what he was told, then sighed and sat down beside Mark. "Master, when they come for us will you do me a favor?"

Mark didn't answer. He continued working, frantically trying to remember how many parts of each ingredient were necessary.

"I would like for you to end my life quickly before they get a chance to cook me. I do not think it would be at all pleasant to be boiled."

"Clean out my pouch, Yonk. You are in charge of keeping track of my things. For now I need to store some of the powder in it. I will keep the rest folded inside this cloth."

Carefully Mark scooped up what he hoped was close to the recipe for the explosive powder and filled his pouch. Then he stood up. "Come, Yonk. The show's about to begin."

It was early morning. The two crept around the rim of the old volcano close to the village. It was quiet. Nothing moved. Mark motioned for Yonk to go for the mounts and then made his way to the hut where the Samatin had taken Sarbo.

There was no guard. Apparently they thought Sarbo was too badly wounded to be a threat.

Mark ducked inside. "Sarbo? Are you here?"

"Of course I am here, infant. What took you so long?"

Mark smiled. Sarbo was lying perfectly still on the floor. "Can you walk?"

"I think so. Help me up."

Leaning on Mark, Sarbo took a wobbly step.

"We must hurry. It will be full daylight soon and they will be looking for us," Mark said.

He half carried Sarbo out the door and across the grounds to the edge of the village, where Yonk was waiting with the beasts and his mount.

"Hello, Master Sarbo. See, you were wrong about me. I have been of great help to you. Look, I found Master Kakon's weapons and have even stolen this extra sword and crossbow. First I—"

"Not now, Yonk." Mark pushed past him. "Help me get him on his mount."

Sarbo was so weak he nearly fell. "Hold him on, Yonk." Mark took the reins and led the animals back toward the tunnel.

A guard was pacing back and forth in front of the opening.

Mark whispered to Yonk, "I'm going to create a diversion. When the guard leaves his post, take Sarbo and the beasts and hurry through the tunnel. I will join you as soon as I can. If I don't come, go on without me. I entrust Sarbo to your care."

Before Yonk could ask any questions Mark slipped away into the darkness.

In minutes a loud explosion ripped the night apart and the guard ran to investigate. Yonk, Sarbo and the beasts disappeared into the tunnel.

The Samatin village sprang to life. Mark crawled to his feet and brushed at his singed eyebrows. His mixture had been more potent than he'd expected. He had poured only a small amount on the ground and tossed a burning stick into it, hoping the sparks would attract the guard's attention. At first nothing had happened. Then it had suddenly caught fire. The force of the explosion was so great it had blown him backward.

Mark ran to the tunnel. He tripped and fell on the slippery rocks as he made his way through the darkness.

There were shouting and the sound of running feet behind him. The Samatin were in the tunnel too, and they were coming fast.

Mark could see light ahead. Hurriedly he dumped out the contents of the rag, then struck his fire rocks together and lit the end of a dry stick he was carrying in his belt. He stepped back and tossed the stick, then turned and leaped into a run.

The explosion was deafening. The walls of the tunnel crumbled. Rock fragments flew everywhere. The blast blew white smoke out of the tunnel and Mark along with it. When he landed he could hear the screams of the men back in the tunnel.

"Master! We are here!" Yonk led the beasts up to him.

Sarbo raised his head. "Well done, Kakon. Well done."

chapter 45

"*Are you sure about this, Sarbo?*" Mark looked down at his friend. He was lying behind his mount on a pole stretcher they had hastily put together.

Sarbo smiled weakly. His face had lost most of its color. "I am sure, Kakon. I am going back to our village to die. The runt will take me. I will have a fine warrior's burial and they will sing many songs about my bravery."

"You are too mean and ornery to die, Sarbo. But I do think that the village is the best place for you. They will tend your wound and soon you will be back to your old annoying self."

"Annoying? Why, if I was not about to die, I would—"

"I know." Mark knelt by the stretcher. "You would teach me to respect my betters. Here." He took off his claw necklace and put it around Sarbo's neck. "I want you to have this. You have been a true friend, Sarbo. No one could ask for better."

Mark stood and turned to Yonk. "Take good care of him.

Follow the directions I have given you. If you get him safely back to the village you will be given your freedom."

"I will do as you ask, master. You can count on me."

"I know I can. And Yonk, if you should meet a girl by the name of Megaan in the village . . . tell her . . ."

"Yes, master?"

"Never mind. You'd better get going. And be careful. There could be other tribes out there."

Mark watched them go until they were only tiny specks on the horizon. He already missed them. His trip to Listra was going to be a lonely one.

Sarbo had given him directions to the ferry that would take him across the great river. After that it was only a few more miles to the Merkon's stronghold.

He would have liked to have the assurance of Sarbo's sword and his vast fighting experience, but even more than that, Sarbo's friendship. Even Yonk's unending chatter would be better than silence.

Mark shrugged the feeling off and sat up straight on his mount. He had been alone before and had survived.

The red Death Sand gradually faded into a soft red dust that grew mostly cactus. Mark let his animal pick its way through the thorny plants.

Sarbo had told him there would be no water here. But if he cut the tops off the larger cactus plants he could find a bitter liquid that would see him through until he reached the river.

Mark stopped only twice to drink. He didn't eat because he was in a hurry and didn't want to take the time to hunt. His mount's flanks were drawing up from exertion and the lack of water. The animal's steps became slower and slower. Finally Mark got off and led the beast until nightfall.

The moonlight gave the night sky an odd yellow glow. Mark stopped to rest. Soon he would continue, hoping to reach the river by morning.

He tied the beast and snuggled down in the warm soft dirt. His mind replayed the events of the previous weeks.

The Merkon had told him of a shaman in Trisad who did not exist. Then they had been attacked on the way to find the imaginary shaman, and the Merkon had been taken captive. Bounty hunters had been offered a reward for Mark's capture. Why? None of it made any sense.

He thought back to Pet, the old man in Trisad who said he was a keeper of knowledge. The stories he had told about the blood sick and the terrible destruction made Mark shudder.

The people had been changed by some catastrophe. They were strange in custom and appearance.

Well, not all of them. Mark drifted off to sleep thinking about how pretty one of them was, especially when she was upset with him.

When he was finished in Listra he would go back and see her one last time before he returned to the dark jungle.

chapter **46**

The big animal lapped up river water for a long time. Mark was worried about letting it have so much. He had read something about overdrinking making animals sick. He ran his hand back and forth in the cool brown water, watching the animal.

"Well, what have we here?"

Mark whirled. A stocky young man with an ugly burn on his face stood behind him, holding a wooden oar.

"Are you not something? Coming here in broad daylight like this. Either you are very brave or you are touched in the head."

Mark jumped to his feet. "I don't know who you think I am but—"

"I have no doubt who you are. You are the young outlaw with the very large price on his head. The word is that you are a bad one indeed. What did you do to get him after you? Normally he does not take such an interest."

"I don't have a clue what you're talking about. I'm simply

looking for the ferry. You wouldn't happen to know if it's up- or downstream, would you?"

"You *are* touched. Do you not realize that everyone in the area has been alerted to look for you? You would be spotted instantly if you tried to cross the river on the ferry. The Merkon has spies everywhere."

"The Merkon?" Mark tried to think. So it was true. The Merkon had offered a reward for his capture. He put his hand on the hilt of his sword. "Are you here to try to collect the bounty?"

The young man gave a wry laugh. "If I was, I could easily have struck you on the head with my oar. Put away your sword, outlaw. I am no friend of the Merkon. It was one of his men who did this to me." He pointed at the burn on his cheek.

Mark relaxed. "Do you know of another way across the river?"

"Maybe. But first you must tell me why you wish to go into the demon's lair. The reward for you holds whether you are dead or alive. What is so significant over there that you would risk your life for it?"

"Answers. I am not an outlaw. The Merkon knows I'm not. He also has information about something that is very important to me. If he is still alive, I have to have it."

"Oh, he is alive, all right. He just recently returned from a very long trip. And he wasted no time getting the word out about you." The young man rubbed his chin. "I have a raft. Your beast will have to swim but I know of a narrow place in the river. Come with me."

Mark hesitated, then grabbed his mount's reins. He wasn't sure whether he could trust this man, but it looked as if he had no choice.

The young man looked back. "What do they call you, outlaw?"

"Some call me Kakon."

"Interesting name. What does it mean?"

"I am told it means 'the second warrior.' "

"Where are you from?"

"A faraway place."

"Closemouthed. I like that. A man can never be too careful. My name is Roan. I live across the river with a small group of murderers and thieves."

Mark stopped. "Is that where we're going?"

"Yes. They are an unruly bunch. But once they find out who you are they will be pleased that you have joined us. Here is the raft. Give me a hand, will you?"

Mark helped him push the raft into the water. "Why do you live with murderers and thieves? You don't seem like the type."

"When the great Merkon puts a mark like this on your face, you are no longer welcome among the true people."

"Why did he do that to you?"

"I used to work for him in the stronghold. I tended the stables as a young boy and worked my way up to become a member of the elite guard. Life could not have been better for me until I met Dansa."

"Dansa?"

"The Merkon's daughter. We were going to run away together. But we were caught by her brother, Mordo. The Merkon branded me as a thief. He would have branded her too, but she denied everything and blamed me." Roan shrugged. "I guess it wasn't true love after all. Now I am banished from Listra. So I hide with my companions in the forest and live by my wits. You are welcome to stay with us."

"Thank you, Roan." Mark stepped onto the raft and pulled his beast to the edge of the water. "I just might take you up on that."

Roan pushed off and began rowing. The beast followed and was soon covered with water except for its head. Roan let the current take them downstream a short distance and then started rowing again until they reached the other side.

A wide man with a flat face, scraggly hair and thick bare feet jumped out of the bushes and caught the rope Roan threw to him. He pulled the raft to shore and helped them hide it in the brush.

"This is Francle. At one time he was the Merkon's chief advisor. That was before he advised something the Merkon did not want to hear and his tongue was cut out."

Mark winced and nodded at the man. "Nice to meet you."

Francle nodded back and reached for the reins of Mark's beast.

Mark jerked them away. "I'll keep it with me, if you don't mind."

The man frowned and moved up the trail in front of them. Roan winked at Mark. "Wise decision. Francle has been known to *borrow* a mount from time to time. He sells them to an old trader across the river."

"So you steal from each other too?"

"Oh no. Only from strangers."

"It's nice to know you draw the line somewhere."

Roan laughed and led the way up a narrow path through stands of tall red trees. "So you claim you are not really an outlaw. You must have done something. What was it? Did you hear or see something you were not supposed to? Perhaps you failed to carry out a mission you were entrusted with."

"It was none of those things. At least I don't think it was. I'm not really sure. To tell you the truth, I think it has something to do with the way I look."

"Ha!" Roan slapped his leg. "That is very funny. The great Merkon wants to arrest you because of your looks." Roan stopped walking and turned to study Mark. "I admit you do look odd. You are very tall, your skin has a pasty look and your eyes are misshapen." He snapped his fingers. "I have it. You are related to the Merkon. I saw him once without his mask. He had those same strange eyes."

This time it was Mark's turn to laugh. "That's not it either. I can't explain right now, but believe me, there's no way I would be related to the Merkon."

"Too bad. It would have made a good story to tell at the fire tonight." Roan stepped through a hedge of brush. "We will not speak from this point on, Kakon. For the next mile or so, the forest is inhabited by the worst kind of beasts. Spies sent from the Merkon to locate our band. Walk only where I walk."

Mark watched Roan slip a knife from his moccasin. He followed suit by reaching for his crossbow and loading one of his arrows.

They had traveled a fair distance when they heard a loud snap and a strange whirring noise. Then came the sound of someone crashing through the brush in their direction.

Mark wanted to hide but Roan stood his ground, poised and ready.

Francle charged out of the brush, motioning excitedly for them to follow him.

A sly grin crept over Roan's face. "Come, Kakon," he whispered. "I think you will enjoy this."

Francle led the way to a clearing and pointed above their heads. Hanging by one foot and trying desperately to free himself from the noose around his foot was one of the Merkon's soldiers. His helmet and sword had fallen to the ground and the skirt of skins he wore had dropped over his head, exposing his bare backside.

"Looks as if one of your traps has caught a varmint, Francle. A rather large one this time. Take care of it. And see if you can find his mount." Roan took a step and stopped. "And Francle, be sure the mount gets back to camp."

"Come, Kakon. Our camp is not far now." Roan led the way through a dense thicket. On the other side he stopped and called out, "Ho, the camp. It is I, Roan, with a distinguished guest."

A voice from the trees answered. "Proceed and welcome to Roan and his guest."

Mark scanned the treetops but couldn't find the owner of the voice. He followed Roan down a narrow ravine, which opened into a small clearing. There were no people, but a nearly smokeless fire burned in the center and a small animal was cooking on a wooden spit.

Armor and swords were stacked up on one side, and a string of beasts was tied to a long rope. One by one, six men stepped out from behind trees and stood in front of them.

"Is this who I think it is?" A man with a scar burned into his face like Roan's looked Mark up and down.

"It is, Jod." Roan held out his hand. "My friends, may I

present the young outlaw, Kakon? I found him on the other side of the river, looking for the ferry."

"The ferry?" A thin man with a shaved head moved close to Mark. "He is a bold rascal. What did he intend to do, take on the company of guards on the bank by himself?"

"That I do not know. All he has told me is that he desires to see the great Merkon on a personal matter."

Jod circled behind them. Mark's hand felt for the release on his crossbow.

Roan touched Mark's shoulder. "Have no fear, my pale new friend." He glared at Jod. "You know better. Kakon is my guest. I told him he would be welcome here. Bring him food and water. Perhaps before this day is over we will all find out how useful we can be to one another."

chapter **47**

"**The stronghold is on the other side of** Listra. It has a high wall that completely encircles it. Inside there is a shelter room for the guards to sleep in and a stable that houses a hundred riding beasts. The main house is like nothing you have ever seen. It has a large hall with a plank floor and behind that more than ten rooms used solely by the Merkon and his family."

Mark didn't comment. He waited for Roan to finish.

"The tribute is kept in one of the back rooms. I have never seen it but one time Dansa told me about it. She described it in detail so I know for certain it is there."

"And you want me to help you break into the stronghold to get it."

"Yes. We have eight good men. You make nine. If we attack at night we will have the element of surprise. And if while you are there you get a chance to handle your business with the Merkon, so much the better. What do you say?"

"I say no."

Jod pulled his sword. "He is a coward, Roan. Let me cut his heart out."

"Let me finish." Mark stood and brushed the crumbs from his clothes. "By the way, thank you for the meal. I haven't eaten in a long time. It is very much appreciated."

Roan raised an eyebrow. "You were saying?"

"Just that I think there is a better way. If the stronghold is guarded as heavily as you say, I don't think you're going to have an easy time sneaking over the wall."

"Go on."

"Suppose they opened the gate for you? Suppose you brought them something the Merkon wants? Not only would you be taken to the tribute room for payment, you would get in without a fight."

"And that something would be . . ."

"Me."

chapter **48**

It was dark. Mark rode in front of a col-
umn of eight armored men. His hands were loosely tied in
front of him and he wore a long cloak of skins to cover his
sword.

"Open the gate," Roan shouted. "We have a prisoner for
the Merkon."

A small iron peephole scraped open. A deep voice called
out, "Identify yourselves and the prisoner."

Roan adjusted the helmet to make sure it covered his face.
He had been a member of the guard long enough to know
what to say. "I am Vagra with the desert company. The
prisoner is the odd-looking outlaw the Merkon has been
searching for. I am here for the reward."

"Wait." The iron peephole slid shut.

In a few minutes the heavy gate creaked open and the
column rode inside.

Mark glanced around. Most of the Merkon's men were in
the sleeping shelter. But the night guards were on duty and

they were stationed every few feet all the way around the wall.

A gate guard took Mark's beast. "So you are the one we have been searching for. Get down. The Merkon wishes to see you immediately." He turned to Roan. "Follow me, Vagra. The Merkon will see that you are well rewarded."

Roan got off his mount and stood between Mark and the guard. "This is my prisoner and I will be the one to deliver him." He reached up and pulled Mark off his beast. Then he turned to his men. "Francle, take care of the animals. The rest of you dismount and give me a hand. This one is bad. Extremely violent and tricky. I do not want him escaping now that we are finally here."

The guard's eyes narrowed. He stiffened but turned, leading the way up the wooden steps into the main house.

Mark was surprised to see how well furnished the great hall was. There were colorful rugs on the floor and benches with cushions. Large murals were painted on the walls and at one end sat a tall, ornately carved chair with a high wooden back.

"So what do you think, Kakon?"

Mark turned. The Merkon and two of his men had entered the room from a side door.

"Of what? The chair, the room—or the way I was brought in here like a dog for crimes I never committed?"

"Still not afraid of me, are you? We'll change that in due time. I'm really glad they brought you in alive. I was hoping they would. I wanted to talk to you."

"I'm listening."

"Unfortunately, so are others." The Merkon waved his

hand. "Guard, take these men and give them a fitting reward. See to it that no one comes in or out of this room until I call."

The guard led Roan and his men out the side door and closed it behind them.

The Merkon walked to the tall chair and sat down. "Now, let's see. Where should I begin?"

"Try telling me why you're so interested in me. And what do you know about the light that brought me here?"

The Merkon sat back. "You are a smart boy. I would have thought you'd have had it all figured out by now."

"The only thing I have figured out is that somehow I am a threat to you and that you have gone to a whole lot of trouble to get me out of the way. You even ambushed your own men on the way to Trisad to get at me. Why?"

The Merkon reached for the strange helmet covering his face and slowly took it off. Mark stared. The Merkon didn't resemble the Tsook or anyone else Mark had run across in this world. Instead he looked more like . . .

"I knew you were smart." The Merkon put his helmet back on. "You're right. I am not from Transall. I am from your time. At least close to it. What year was it when you came through the warp?"

"You—You came here through the light? Then you know where it is and how to get back."

"Now, why would I want to do that? I knew one day someone else was bound to find the warp. It was just a question of time. I was hoping that it would be far in the future, however, long after my kingdom had ended. When I heard about you I knew something had to be done."

212

"What are you talking about?" Mark asked. "We can work together to get back."

"But that's just it. I don't want to go back. I am the ruler of the universe here. These people are putty in my hands. Ignorant fools. These savages think I am the wisest, most powerful being that ever existed."

Mark sat on one of the benches. "That's another thing I don't understand. How did all this happen? What caused these changes?"

"From what I have been able to determine, there was a massive plague from a strain of virus much like the Ebola carried by African monkeys. It was very contagious and apparently an awfully painful way to die. If you contracted it, blood seeped out of every opening in your body until nothing was left. Scientists tried everything but they couldn't find a cure. It swept over the world, killing at least seventy percent of the population. The infrastructure broke down, whole countries were virtually depopulated and for several generations the virus kept the population so low there could be no progress. Finally, when the virus at last died out, so much time had passed that everything useful had been forgotten; the human race had to start over. It must have been something to see."

"The virus didn't cause the changes in the people and plant life. What did that?"

"That has been a little harder to piece together. The best I can tell, when major powers like the United States began to crumble, the nuclear weapons were taken over by terrorists who shot them off at will. Everything on Earth underwent a tremendous chemical change and over the next two thousand years only the strongest of any species survived."

"What about the light?"

"The light is a time warp, a freak of nature. I found it in the desert in the 1980s when I escaped from a prison detail in Arizona. It was unbelievable. I wanted out and, presto, I was so far out they could never find me."

"Don't you want to go back? What about your family and friends?"

"Weren't you listening? I told you I was in prison. I had no family. I had nothing. Here I have everything. And I don't intend to let you take it away from me."

"I don't want to take anything. All I want to do is find that light."

"And what if you never find it? Soon you will start talking and teaching these people. I saw the armor you had made. What else have you taught them? Reading? How to build weapons? I can't allow that. Soon they might rise up and use it all against me."

"You're a lunatic. I'm walking out of here."

The Merkon unsheathed his sword. "I don't think so."

Mark threw his cape off and reached for his own sword. He had it out barely in time to parry a blow aimed at his head.

"Someone has taught you well, boy. But not well enough." The Merkon came at him from the side.

Mark leaped away but the tip of the blade ripped through his shirt. He whirled, bringing his sword around hard. The Merkon was ready. He jumped and swung again, pushing Mark backward onto one of the benches.

"Now you are going to die and no one from either world will ever know what happened to you." The Merkon forced Mark flat on his back.

"Before I kill you, Kakon, you should know that you never would have found the light. It strikes where it wants, randomly. There is no predictable pattern." He pushed his blade closer to Mark's face, the sharp edge inches from his throat.

Mark shoved him but the Merkon was too strong. Then Mark raised his knees and kicked. The Merkon lost his balance and Mark rolled off the bench.

Mark scrambled to his feet and started swinging. He brought his sword up the way Sarbo had taught him and sliced the Merkon's stomach. A red stain appeared on the man's shirt. The Merkon stumbled and gasped for breath. Mark pressed in, hacking and probing, and with a wild sweep knocked the sword from the Merkon's hand.

"Now we will see who's going to die." Mark raised his sword.

A tremendous explosion shook the building. Roan and Jod burst through the side door, each carrying a bulging sack.

Roan winked at him. "If you are almost done with your business, Kakon, I suggest we leave now. Francle used a little more of the powder than you told him to. Half the wall on the east side is gone and all their beasts have run off."

Mark slowly lowered his sword. "I am finished. This . . . man . . . has nothing I want."

"Surely you are not going to leave him alive?" Jod asked incredulously.

"His wounds are fatal. Let him die the slow, painful death he deserves." Mark reached for the Merkon's helmet and placed it on his own head. "Francle will be waiting for us."

The courtyard was in chaos. The Merkon's men were

running everywhere. Francle and the others were already mounted.

Mark took some of the powder and poured it on the steps of the stronghold. When he was a good distance away, he grabbed one of the torches and threw it onto the powder. The blast blew logs and men everywhere. The whole front of the building vanished.

Roan handed Mark his reins. "Not a bad night's work, outlaw."

Mark jumped on his mount. "Let's ride."

chapter 49

It was early morning. Mark built up the fire and sat staring into it. There was no question that the Merkon was insane. He was so power hungry he couldn't see past himself. It had been a waste of time to come to Listra.

Mark sighed. For now, he and the band of robbers were safe deep in the forest, and there were lookouts posted in case the Merkon's men tried to come after them.

The large sacks of tribute still sat where Roan and his men had dropped them the previous night. Everyone was so worn out from the long ride that they were sleeping on the ground, still wearing their weapons.

Jod had been furious with Mark for not killing the Merkon and Mark couldn't really explain to himself why he hadn't done it. Maybe it had something to do with finally finding a real link to his own time.

Footsteps sounded behind him. He turned to see Roan coming to join him at the fire.

"You are up early, Kakon. What is the matter? Can you not wait to receive your share of the booty?"

Mark threw a stick in the fire. "To tell you the truth, I'm not much interested. You guys can split my share."

Roan cocked his head. "You are different from anyone I have ever met. Not just in the way you look but in the way you think." The young man warmed his hands. "You can trust me with your story, Kakon. I will understand."

"My story is that the Merkon considers me a threat to his kingdom. And I thought he had some information I needed. It turns out we were both wrong."

"What will you do now? He is certain to send men to hunt for you."

"I really don't know. I guess the only thing left to do is to go on searching for answers. Maybe I'll go back to my village for a while. There is a girl there . . ."

Roan sat up. "A girl? How can I help? My men are at your disposal."

A loud birdcall shrieked through the morning air.

Roan jumped to his feet. "The lookout. Someone is in the forest."

Mark followed Roan through the trees to a thick stand of brush, where they crouched and waited. In minutes a large column of men in heavy armor rode by.

When they were well out of sight Roan motioned for Mark to return to the camp with him.

"Did you see the man riding at the head of the column, Kakon?"

"Not really. Who is he?"

"That was Mordo, the Merkon's son. He is even more ruthless than his father."

At camp everybody was moving. Francle, Jod and the others had been awakened by the birdcall. They had doused the fire and were preparing to leave.

"Who was it?" Jod asked. "Do they already look for us?"

Roan nodded. "It appears so. And Mordo is leading them. We had better move farther back into the woods."

"You and your men go on ahead," Mark said. "I think it's a good time for me to be going my own way."

"What is this?" Jod asked. "You would leave us without your share of the spoils?"

"He has to go, Jod." Roan slapped Mark on the back. "He does not have time for riches. He has a girl waiting for him somewhere."

Mark started to explain but then decided not to. Instead he untied his animal. "I have enjoyed your company. You are welcome to make camp with me anytime."

"And you are always welcome in ours." Roan handed him an extra water pouch. "Take this. You will need it if you are going back through the desert." He watched Mark climb onto his beast. "I hope you find what you are looking for, Kakon."

Mark waved and turned around. "Me too, Roan. Me too."

chapter **50**

The trip back across the desert had been uneventful and lonely. Mark had deliberately stayed away from Trisad and visited the sparse water holes only after dark.

It had given him time to think. If it was true that the blue light struck randomly, then there was very little hope of his ever returning to his family and his own time. He knew he would still search for it but finding it would be like looking for a single grain of sand on a beach. It was time to face the fact that he had to make a life in this world.

There was just one place he wanted to go now. Back to the village. It was the only semblance of a home that he had on this strange new Earth. He wanted to go there and see all the familiar faces he had left behind. And then he wanted to sleep. Sleep for a week.

He rode with slack reins and let his beast have its head. They were getting close. The red valley loomed before him. It was all he could do not to break into a run.

A hunting horn sounded from behind a boulder on the

mountain. The sound made Mark smile. It was good to be back.

As he approached the village wall there was another blast from the tower horn, identifying him as a friend.

Mark rode through the gates and up the main street. Everything was just as he'd left it. Tybor the blacksmith was busy working in his lean-to and the people were attending to their daily chores.

Everyone waved and shouted greetings as he passed. Tybor wanted to know what had taken him so long to come back.

A cloud of dust came flying at him from the other end of the street. A boy on a gray beast pulled up in front of him. "I knew it was you," he burst out.

Mark squinted in mock disbelief. "Could this be Barow? I can't believe it. You've grown into a warrior while I was gone."

Barow sat up a little straighter on his mount. "It will not be long now, Kakon." He turned and rode beside Mark. "I have taken care of all your things as you asked me to. I think you will be pleased."

"Mark. You are back." Leeta waved at him from Tanta's storehouse. She put down her supplies and hurried over. "It is so good to see you. I was worried because you have been away so long. Any news about the light?"

"The light strikes where it wants to. Finding it is a hopeless dream. That part of my life is over. I've decided to put it behind me and get on with my new life. How have things been with you?"

"Good. I have become accustomed to living with the Tsook. I have been put in charge of many things. One of

221

them is keeping an eye on your young friend, Barow. He gives me fits, though, and it is almost impossible to watch him now that you have given him that beast."

Mark winked at Barow. "Every warrior needs a beast."

"*Hummp.* You are a bad influence." Leeta pretended to be upset. Then she smiled. "I must get the things from the storehouse. I will see you later. We will have a long talk."

"Sounds good." Mark turned to Barow. "How is Sarbo? Did he make it?"

"Come and see for yourself, Kakon." Barow urged the gray into a lope. Mark followed him around the storehouse to a large cabin near the village wall.

Yonk was sitting on the porch carving a stick. When he saw Mark he jumped up. "Master, it is you. Wait until Sarbo hears." He darted into the cabin.

In seconds Sarbo stepped out the front door. He had a wide grin on his face. "So you have returned. It is probably because you found you were unable to finish your quest without me."

"It's a long story. After I've rested I'll tell it." Mark looked at his friend. "It's good to see you well. I thought you said you were coming back here to die."

Sarbo cleared his throat. "I never said that. You must have heard me wrong."

"No, that is what you said, Master Sarbo." Yonk squeezed past him and came out on the porch. "In fact, all the way across the desert you talked about being buried and the songs you wanted."

Sarbo made a face. "As you can see, I still have not figured out a way to get the runt to shut up. Even giving him his freedom did not work. Now he thinks he can talk all the more."

Mark turned. "I'll be back, Sarbo. There is someone else I need to see."

"Who is that, Kakon? Can I come too?" Barow trotted down the street after him.

"I suppose. After all, we are going to your house."

"My house? Oh, you want to see my father. I think he is in the field today."

Mark didn't comment. He turned off the main street and rode up the dirt path to Dagon's cabin. He slid down and handed his reins to Barow. "Take care of my mount. It's had a long hard trip."

Mark waited until Barow led the animal to water and then knocked on the front door.

It opened wide.

"Kakon!" Megaan exclaimed as she stepped outside. "I am so glad to see you. Sarbo led us to believe you could be gone for quite some time."

"Are you really glad to see me?"

A soft look came into her eyes. "Of course I am. I was not sure if I would ever see you again."

"And would that have bothered you?"

Megaan frowned. "Did you come back just to fight with me?"

"Actually"—Mark stepped closer and put his arms around her—"I came back for this." He leaned down and kissed her.

223

chapter 51

"Is it true that you are going to marry my sister?" Barow had a look of disgust on his face.

"Who told you that?" Mark measured off one corner of his land and pounded a stake into the ground.

"Everybody in the village has been talking about it for weeks. Is it true?"

"To tell you the truth, I have been thinking about it. See, if I marry Megaan then you and I will be brothers. I thought it might be worth it just for that. What do you think?"

"I think you are crazy. Nothing would be worth marrying Megaan. She is too bossy and mean."

"Did I hear someone talking about me?" Megaan said, coming up behind them.

Mark turned. He put down the rest of his stakes and wiped his hands on his pants. "Barow here was just giving me a rundown of all your faults. He thinks it would be a big mistake to marry you. You being so hardheaded and all."

Megaan folded her arms. "Barow, Grandmother wants you at the cabin. She needs help with the vegetables."

Barow's lip went out. "You made that up just to get rid of me."

"Get going," Megaan ordered.

They watched him climb onto the gray and ride away. Mark faced Megaan and took one of her hands. "Barow says everyone in the village is talking about us."

Megaan flushed. "It is the way of the Tsook. They look forward to all celebrations."

"And ours is going to be the greatest." Mark took her other hand. "I just wish I had some crops planted. Things might be a little tough for us for a while."

Megaan's chin went up. "I am not worried. You are a good hunter. We will not go hungry."

Her compliment filled him. He had thought himself too young for this, too young for marriage or being with another person, but it all seemed so . . . so right. According to the Tsook customs, both of them were already past marriage age. "Speaking of hunting, your grandmother asked me to bring back some fresh meat for her today. If I don't get started it will be dark before I get back. Why don't you come with me?"

Megaan pulled her hands away. "You know I cannot leave the village and be alone with you. It is not done."

"You're alone with me now." His arm went around her shoulders. "And I remember a time not so long ago that you rode out to look for me when I was wounded. We were alone then too."

"That was different. We were younger then." She tried to pull away. "Kakon. You will embarrass my family."

Mark gave her a quick kiss on the forehead. "We can't have that, now, can we?" He untied his beast and swung on.

"Tell your grandmother I will be back soon. If I don't find anything for her stew pot today I will keep looking until I do."

"Kakon."

"Yes?"

"I think it would not be good for you to be gone too long."

Mark sat back. "And I think Barow was right. You are bossy." He kicked his mount into a run.

The dirt clod missed him by only a few inches.

chapter 52

Mark settled down next to his small fire. He was wishing he hadn't been so greedy but had gone ahead and taken the two rabbit creatures he had seen earlier. Because he had wanted to impress Megaan and her family he'd let them go and searched for larger game. But he hadn't found any.

Close to dark he had come upon the fresh tracks of a tragg, a large elklike animal. But now it was too late to track it. He would have to try to pick up the trail again in the morning.

He leaned back on his elbows. Life in this world wasn't so bad. He did what he wanted and went where he pleased. He was a Tsook warrior and in a few months he would have a wife. They could start a family.

He had deliberately squeezed out all thoughts of his other life. He calculated that he was somewhere close to seventeen now. In this world that was a grown man. Sarbo still teased him but treated him with more respect than he had before.

Dagon had seemed pleased that Mark had chosen to ask

Megaan. In the months since he had been back they'd had a long talk about Mark's run-in with the Merkon and decided that if the Overlord or any of his men ever came to the village again they would simply be told that Mark had never returned.

Mark closed his eyes and was about to drift off to sleep when he heard a branch break. Silently he reached for the crossbow near his fingertips and rolled away from the fire into the shadows.

"Ho, the fire. I am a weary traveler looking for food and a place to spend the night."

Mark stayed in the shadows. "Come forward and lay down your weapons."

A man wearing armor walked out in the opening and leaned down to place his sword on the ground. When he did there was a rustling in the brush behind Mark.

He rolled but it was too late. A large man jumped on him and wrestled the crossbow out of his hands. Mark struggled but it was no use. He was pinned solidly to the ground.

The other man picked up his sword and walked over. "Well, well, what have we here? It appears to be our young outlaw. Let him up, Francle. I think we know this one."

"Roan?" Mark scrambled out from under his attacker. "Is that you? And Francle? What are you doing way out here?"

"Looking for you." Roan helped him to his feet and Francle patted his shoulder apologetically. "Of course we never expected to find you camping out in the hills. Why are you not in your village keeping company with your girl? Did she throw you over?"

"No. In fact, we're getting married in a few months. I'm just out hunting."

"Not having much luck, by the looks of things."

"Never mind about that. You said you were looking for me. Why?"

Roan walked to the fire and sat down. "I am afraid we come with bad news. Jod and the others are all dead. Mordo caught them at the trader's on the other side of the river. He killed everyone, including the old trader and his family. Francle and I were guarding the camp or we would have been with them."

"I'm sorry, Roan." Mark sat beside him. "Look, the two of you can come live with me. I have a good cabin in the village."

"There is more, Kakon. Mordo has taken his father's place. You wounded the Merkon so severely that he stays in his rooms now. Mordo has vowed revenge on you. He burned the forest looking for you and now he and most of his father's army are on their way here to find you."

Mark swallowed. It took a few seconds for the impact of Roan's message to sink in. Mordo was determined to kill him. And he would stop at nothing to see that it was done.

"I have put my village in danger, Roan. I never should have come back." Mark began kicking dirt on the fire. "I have to warn them and then I will leave . . . forever."

"Where will you go, Kakon? The Merkon's son will hunt you no matter where you run."

Mark stopped. "I will run only so long as it pleases me. When the Merkon's son is in my territory, then I will fight."

"Now that sounds more like it!" Roan said. "It just so happens that at the moment Francle and I are homeless. We would be more than happy to come along."

Francle nodded vigorously.

Mark shook his head. "It is my fight. I can't ask you to risk your lives."

"Who is asking? Besides, I owe Mordo. He is the one who turned me in. Remember?"

"You are a good friend, Roan." Mark's voice was dangerously cold and even. "But this is something I have to do alone."

chapter 53

"*Please try to understand, Megaan. I'm* leaving because I care for you and your people. As long as I am here you are all in danger. Mordo will burn the whole village and kill everyone in it. He doesn't care whom he hurts as long as it gets him closer to me."

"But our warriors will fight for you. They have taken a blood oath. My father says we will fight to the last man if necessary."

"Don't you see? If I leave here no one else has to die. There's no other way."

"Let him go, Megaan." Leeta stepped out on the porch. "Kakon has chosen the right way. If you care for him you will not hold him back."

Megaan buried her face in his chest. "When this is over . . ."

Mark held her close. "When it is over."

Barow brought up the silver mount. "You have much food and supplies, Kakon. Your pouch with the black exploding powder is wrapped to keep it dry."

"Thank you, Barow." Mark took the reins. "I'm going to need you to take care of things for me again. Especially watch out for your sister. Even if she is a little hardheaded and bossy." He smiled down at Megaan.

Dagon stood up from the bench where he was sitting with Sarbo, Roan and Francle. "I wish you much luck, Kakon. And remember, this will always be your home."

Mark nodded. "I'll remember."

"Good-bye, infant," Sarbo bellowed. "I have decided I do not care for funerals much. Come back alive."

"I'll see what I can do."

Roan cocked his head. "Are you sure Francle and I cannot come? We would welcome the opportunity to pay Mordo for his treachery."

"Not this time." Mark let Megaan go and jumped onto his mount. He gave them all one last long look. He tried to imprint their faces on his memory.

It was time to leave.

A warning blast sounded from the tower, immediately followed by two more. Mark pulled up. He had waited too long. Mordo was already there.

"I'll lead them away," Mark shouted. He sank his heels into the mount's sides and raced down the road.

Two warriors were scrambling to close the front gate. Mark darted through the narrow opening and stopped on the other side. In the distance Mordo and his army were marching toward the village.

Mark stood by the wall and waited until he was sure they could see him clearly. Then he headed for the mountain.

It worked. Mordo and his army broke into a run and came after him.

Mark flew up the hill, jumping and crashing through the brush. Years ago, when he had tried to escape slavery this way, he hadn't known where he was going. Now he did. He knew exactly where he was taking them. He only hoped they would follow.

Behind him he could hear orders being shouted and the sound of running animals. Once he was over the crest of the hill he slipped into the valley below and rode down the canyon in the open to make sure they didn't lose sight of him.

An arrow whistled past his head. Mark turned off into a thicket. There was an old path that was almost overgrown. He had found it the month before when he was out hunting.

The army had to slow down and travel single file through the thorny brush. By the time they made it through the tangle, Mark was already up on the next hill watching them. He let his beast rest and waited for them to regroup.

He counted them. Forty men. Not an extremely large army but enough to overwhelm most villages.

Someone spotted him on the hillside and yelled. At once the chase was on.

Mark moved the silver beast into a trot. If they kept on like this, by nightfall he would have them well away from the village. After that he wasn't really sure what his plans were. The main thing was to keep them on unfamiliar territory and keep them moving.

Mordo was more than willing to cooperate. He was relentless in the chase. Twice he thought he and his men had Mark cornered, only to find that the warrior had escaped from under their noses.

They followed him until the daylight vanished, then

Mordo reluctantly ordered them to make a cold camp on the side of a mountain.

Mark made camp too, in the rocks just above them, where he could keep an eye on their activities. He slept for a few hours, then made sure his mount was tied securely and crept down to their camp. He lay watching for a long time, until he was certain the guard watching their mounts was asleep. Then he collected the bridles from their beasts, which wandered off as soon as they were untied. He dumped the bridles into a nearby deep pit.

He had planned to relieve the group of some of their supplies as well, but one of the loose mounts knocked over a small dead tree, awakening the men.

Mark returned to his own camp, gathered his things and circled to the bottom of the mountain to wait for morning.

chapter 54

Now that most of Mordo's men were on foot, Mark didn't have to hurry. He led them along slowly and used the time to plan.

They had been traveling for two days and were headed straight for the jungle. At first Mark was worried that Mordo might not continue the chase, but Roan had been right. The Merkon's son was not about to let anything stop him from getting revenge.

On the outskirts of the jungle Mark got off his mount and removed his supply bags and weapons. Where he was going now was no place for the big animal. The beast would not be able to walk through the tangled trees and vines.

He stroked the animal's soft neck. "You go back to the village—they'll take care of you there." He stepped back and slapped the beast hard on the rear. It jumped and then bolted off in the direction they had come from.

Mark shouldered his crossbow and supplies and entered the jungle. He was careful to leave footprints for Mordo and his men to find.

The screaming birds immediately began making a fuss. Something about the sound made him smile.

He made a wide circle, deliberately avoiding water. Mordo and his men would have to find their own. He wasn't going to show them where it lay.

Mark walked to the burned-out village of the arrow people. There was nothing left except a few blackened spots on the ground. He stood in the middle of the space, remembering what it had been like. He had been so glad to find people back then. Leeta and her tribe had been his first contacts in Transall. They had taught him that in this world, war and killing weren't a part of life, they were life.

He walked to the place where the arrow people had cut the path out of the jungle. It was completely overgrown now. Mark found a good spot to hide his supplies and took his water pouch to see if the stream was still there.

After he had found the water, he gathered his things and headed deeper into the jungle. He wanted Mordo to follow him, but from here on he would make it more difficult.

Occasionally he left footprints and broke off twigs but he moved faster than before. He wanted to get to the dark jungle and have a chance to prepare before the army got there.

It started raining. Mark remembered how it used to rain suddenly here. A clap of thunder broke the silence and the drops flooded down in sheets.

He knew how to stay dry by sticking close to the broad-leafed trees, but as he traveled deeper into the jungle he didn't feel the rain at all. It could not penetrate the heavy overgrowth.

He passed through the clearing where he had killed the Howling Thing and went on to the large pool. He was careful not to leave any sign that he had been there. When he left he would cover his tracks so that Mordo and his men would not find the water.

There was a rabbit creature watering at the edge. Mark moved closer until he could see his reflection. The young man looking back at him was a stranger. He had powerful shoulders and a full chest. His hair hung to the middle of his back and his tanned-hide clothing fit closely.

So this was what the years had done to him. He liked it. The whisker-stubbled face looking back at him was a good one, capable and strong. A thought flashed through his mind. If he had not come to Transall he probably would have looked entirely different.

He knelt and scooped up a handful of the cool water. Then he carefully backtracked to the trail he was creating for Mordo's men.

Finally he made it to the meadow at the edge of the dark jungle. This was where he had spent those first critical months learning how to survive. He wondered at the thought of it. It had seemed hopeless back then. Now he could exist anywhere he chose. The animals and the elements were no longer a threat. In a strange way they had become his friends.

Something stirred in the bushes. Mark knew without looking what it was. A buffalo creature had picked up his scent and was looking for him. He stood completely still and waited for it to give up and go away.

Then he moved across the meadow to the spot where he

had built his tree house. The jungle had taken it over. His ladder was still there, and he hacked away at the vines until he could climb it.

The floor of his old house had fallen through. He looked up to the top branches, half expecting to see the little white monkey-bear, Willie, that had been his friend during those rough times.

The thunder rumbled again. He could hear the rain pelting the tops of the trees. Before he climbed down he stripped several long pieces of bark off the weathered branches he had used to make the floor of his tree house and tucked them under his arm.

The dark jungle still unnerved him. He stepped into the shadows and let his eyes adjust to the dim light. If Mordo and his men were smart they would not follow him here. It was a dangerous place even when you knew your way around.

Mark tied long vines across the trail at ankle height in a few strategic places. Then he hid his pieces of dry bark. Later he would pour some of his black powder on them.

He tested a nearby hanging vine and quickly, almost effortlessly, climbed it. In the top branches of the tree he tied his supply bags to a limb.

The clicking started.

Mark grabbed some tree rocks, crouched on the branch and waited for the monkey-bears to appear. He had played this trick on them years before.

They assembled in the tree to his right. Mark remained motionless until they were about to attack him, expecting him to walk by on the ground below.

Then Mark jumped up, growled and tossed the rocks at them. He laughed as they raced for cover in the jungle.

One little white creature stayed behind. Mark stared into its eyes. "Willie? Is that you?"

For a moment it looked as if the monkey-bear might stay. Mark held his hand out. Suddenly it whirled and raced after the others into the safety of darkness.

"I guess it's been too long," Mark muttered. He swung to the ground and walked out of the dark jungle. There was no sign of Mordo and his men. He didn't understand. He had practically blazed a trail for them to follow. They should be here by now.

He checked his supply of arrows and rested his hand on the hilt of his sword. There was nothing to do but try to find them.

He took a step and a tree rock hit him in the center of the back. Mark turned. A monkey-bear was sitting on the ground just outside the shadows, looking perfectly innocent.

Mark picked up the rock and tossed it back. Like lightning, the monkey-bear reached up and caught it.

"Willie?" Mark sat down and waited for the creature to come closer. It took its time but finally it was standing close.

Mark gave the signal to climb on his back. Without hesitation Willie leaped on his shoulders and threw his arms around Mark's neck.

"Good to see you," Mark said.

Willie chattered something and Mark reached around and stroked his head. "You wait here. I have to go check on something. We'll get reacquainted when I come back."

Mark set him on the ground. Willie chattered a scolding

that followed Mark across the meadow. It reminded him of the last time he had left his little friend.

Except for the usual sounds, the jungle was quiet. This baffled Mark. He was sure he had left a trail they could follow. Where were they?

He backtracked to the clearing where he had killed the Howling Thing. There was no sign of the army. Then, instead of going back through the burned-out village, Mark cut across to the spot where he thought the army would enter.

It was almost dark and he could see campfires outside the jungle. Apparently the men had decided not to come in after him.

Mark crept closer and hid behind the trunk of a large red tree. He could see Mordo pacing back and forth with a scowl on his face. Another soldier was loudly complaining that the small troop he had sent into the jungle to do some scouting ought to be back by now.

So that's it, Mark thought. Mordo wasn't sure he wanted to go into the jungle. Instead he had sent in a scouting expedition. Well, that wasn't good enough. Mark backed into the shadows. Tomorrow he would think of a way to convince Mordo to join him.

chapter 55

The heavy explosion rocked the quiet morn-
ing. Three men who had been sleeping too close to the fire
when Mark had tossed his homemade bomb were hurled
sideways by the blast.

Dust billowed and the camp came alive in seconds. One
soldier spotted a tall running figure. "There he goes!" he
shouted to the others.

"After him!" Mordo ordered. "A sack of tribute to the man
who kills the outlaw."

Mark darted from tree to tree, allowing them only brief
glimpses of him. When he was sure they had taken the bait,
he headed straight for the dark jungle.

In one of the small clearings he heard a buffalo creature
snorting. It had blood on its horns and face and was busy
tossing what looked like the remains of one of the scouts in
the air.

Mark shuddered and looked away. He had other things to
think about. It made him uncomfortable to know that
Mordo's scouts were somewhere out in front of him.

Behind him he could hear Mordo's men coming. He circled the clearing and waited on the other side. The army startled the buffalo creature. It pawed the ground and charged.

A dozen arrows sank into the beast's head and sides but it kept coming. It gored one soldier and would have kept fighting if Mordo hadn't thrust his sword through its heart.

The creature fell to one knee and then toppled over, dead. Mordo didn't stop. He ordered the rest to keep searching for Mark.

Mark deliberately made noise in the brush and then slipped away. When he neared the red meadow in front of the dark jungle he stopped to watch and listen. There was no sign of the scouting party.

He crossed the meadow and waited in the shadows near his old tree house. He didn't wait long.

Mordo and his men stepped out of the brush and scanned the trees. One of the soldiers began to scream. He had stepped on a colony of fire bugs. The warrior rolled on the ground, trying to scrape them off.

Mordo kept moving. Mark darted out of the shadows long enough to be seen briefly, then moved back inside the dark jungle.

He shimmied up a vine and swung to a tree branch. Mordo's army marched into the darkness after him.

Using the vines, Mark swung from tree to tree until he could drop to the spot where he had left his dry tree bark. He quickly poured out some of his powder, placed the bark in two strategic places and swung back up into one of the tall trees.

The birds screeched loudly, announcing the army's arrival.

Next came the clicking. The monkey-bears greeted the strangers with their usual bombardment of tree rocks.

Mark sat patiently on a tree branch with his crossbow loaded.

Mordo continued to lead his men through the dark jungle. He cursed and threatened Mark with what he would do to him.

Mark laughed scornfully and called down, "You have to catch me first, Mordo."

Mordo searched the treetops for the source of the laughter. Suddenly he and the men leading the column tripped on one of the vines Mark had tied. They fell face first into the swamp of quicksand.

It was so dark that several others behind them stumbled into the trap, not realizing where they were until it was too late. Their heavy armor made fighting their way out impossible.

The remaining soldiers scattered and tried to leave the way they had come in. Mark sent a fire arrow into the first pile of powder. It exploded and sent several men flying. Before the others had time to think, he shot a second arrow.

Only a handful of Mordo's men were left. Mark imitated the chilling call of the Howling Thing.

They started running.

chapter 56

Mark sat under his old tree house, sharing tree rocks with Willie. Yesterday he had followed the frightened remnant of the Merkon's army to make sure they left the jungle.

He felt free again. Now he could go back to his village and get on with his life. He patted Willie's head. "How would you like to come with me, boy? Barow will love you."

Thinking about going home made him gulp down the rest of his tree-rock juice and gather his things. If he hurried he could make it to the valley in less than three days.

"Well, how about it?" Mark gave Willie the signal to climb up. "Are you coming?"

The monkey-bear clicked loudly and then jumped on Mark's back.

"That's more like it." Mark shifted his load and started across the meadow.

He was almost to the other side when he heard an awful whirring sound and something ripped into his arm.

It was an arrow. Pain tore through his body. Four o

Mordo's men stepped out from behind trees with their weapons aimed at him.

The scouting party. Mark had completely forgotten about them. They obviously didn't know that Mordo was dead and the rest of the army was scattered.

Mark pretended to raise his hands in surrender and then abruptly dived into the cover of some trees. Willie rolled off as Mark hit the ground. The little monkey-bear climbed the nearest tree, clicking in terror.

Mark made it to his feet and started running. The scouts were right behind him. He crashed through the jungle, not caring which direction he was taking. His only thought was to get away.

He couldn't shake them. His arm was going numb and he felt weak. He kept running, dodging to the right and left.

A loud clap of thunder crashed through the air. The sky lit up with flashes of lightning. Mark ran through the pouring rain with Mordo's men now only yards behind him.

He spotted a boulder to his left and sprinted toward it. If he could just reach it he could use it for cover. He half fell behind it, reached for an arrow and slid his crossbow off his arm.

His wounded arm was too weak to pull the string back. The scouts were pounding toward him. With all the strength he could muster he dragged himself up on the boulder. He pulled out his sword and prepared to leap down on them.

Lightning struck the boulder, sending balls of electricity shooting in all directions. A tube of blue light enveloped Mark and brutally shook his body.

He could feel himself falling.

♦ ♦ ♦

Mark could hear people standing over him, talking. He felt for his sword. Somehow he had to stand and fight. He was determined to take down a few more of Mordo's men before he died.

Groggily he rose to his feet, swinging his sword. He heard screaming and the sound of people calling to him in a strange language.

He focused. In front of him was a strange little fountain. He was no longer in the jungle. Instead he was inside some type of building. The people staring at his clothes and weapons were not from Transall.

A small boy stepped out of the crowd. "Mister, do you need a doctor? I think there's one here in the mall."

Mark pulled the arrow out of the fleshy part of his arm. There was no wound. He looked up at the people.

The little boy had spoken to him in English.

This was his time.

His world.

The blue light had brought him back.

EPILOGUE

Twenty Years Later

"*Dr. Harrison. Dr. Mark Harrison, report* to the second floor."

The voice continued to boom over the intercom.

Mark felt someone jostle his elbow. He looked up from his microscope. "What is it, Karen? Did you find something?"

The young lab assistant smiled. "They're calling you again, Dr. Harrison." She pointed to the intercom.

Mark looked at his watch. "Oh, great. Looks like I'm late for the board meeting again. Get my briefcase, will you? And a copy of that data we were working on this morning."

"It's all here." Karen handed him the case. "Don't forget your tie."

Mark fumbled in his pocket for the wrinkled clip-on. "I hate these things."

"I know. But you *are* trying to make an impression."

Mark sighed. "Right. Maybe this time I'll convince them." He headed for the door.

"Good luck, Doctor. We're all rooting for you."

Mark waved and disappeared through the door.

A dark-haired young man in a white lab coat walked over. "Do you think he has a chance for the grant money?"

Karen shrugged. "I hope so. He's obsessed with finding a cure. He's already come up with several possible vaccines for the virus. But he has to convince the government that these diseases are a matter of global importance."

"He's a strange one. Last night, when he did the final tests on the new Ebola virus inoculations, he looked at the ceiling and whispered, 'Megaan, this is for you,' or something like that. I mean, what's a megaan? Weird . . ."

"He's all right," Karen said. "I think he just needs a break from work. Some friends of mine and I are planning a hike in the desert this weekend through the Magruder Missile Range. Maybe I'll invite him to come along."

"The doc?"

"Yeah. Why not?"

"He's such a bookworm. I doubt he'd last a day out there in the wild."

"I don't know. I think he might surprise you. There's something about him. Have you noticed? It's a look he gets sometimes, almost like he's . . ."

"What?"

"I can't quite put my finger on it. But it's like he's . . . almost savage."

"Ha! The doc is as tame as they come. And if you decide to invite him to go, you guys had better take it real easy on him."

"He'll be fine." Karen laughed. "It's just a hike in the desert. What could happen?"

GARY PAULSEN is the distinguished author of many critically acclaimed books for young people, including three Newbery Honor books: *The Winter Room, Hatchet* and *Dogsong.* His novel *The Haymeadow* received the Western Writers of America Golden Spur Award. Among his newest Delacorte Press books are *My Life in Dog Years, Sarny: A Life Remembered* (a companion to *Nightjohn*), *The Schernoff Discoveries, Brian's Winter* (a companion to *Hatchet*), *Father Water, Mother Woods: Essays on Fishing and Hunting in the North Woods,* and the first three books about Francis Tucket's adventures in the Old West. Gary Paulsen has also published fiction and nonfiction for adults. He and his wife, the painter Ruth Wright Paulsen, live in New Mexico and on the Pacific Ocean.

Books by Gary Paulsen
available from Macmillan
